THE TIDWELL BRAND

To Rose-Mary Rumbley —

R. J. Stepp

P. 79

R. J. STEPP

outskirtspress

DENVER, COLORADO

Outskirts Press, Inc.
http://www.outskirtspress.com

ISBN: 978-1-4787-1740-9

Outskirts Press and the "OP" logo are trademarks belonging to Outskirts Press, Inc.

PRINTED IN THE UNITED STATES OF AMERICA

Chapter One

Little Rock

The War Between the States had been over for more than a month and the memories of the battles he had been in were burned permanently into his mind. It was still difficult for him to believe he had lost many of his closest friends in a battle that took place three days after General Lee had signed surrender papers in Virginia.

It was hot and the sun seemed to burn the land with a dry, dusty breeze that made it hard to breathe. He pulled a piece of what used to be a shirt from his pocket, took off his hat and wiped the sweat that ran in rivulets down his darkly tanned face. He smoothed back an irritating lock of dark brown hair and swore he would get a much needed haircut in the next town he came upon. He was on his long journey home and wanted to get there as quickly as possible, but knew he must take care not to over extend the General. The General had carried him through many battles and had never been far from his side. He knew the General was an extraordinary horse and when he got home as a reward for his loyalty, would turn him out and let him just be a horse.

The long hot day was turning to evening and the shadows of the tall, deep green pines were growing long and he knew it was time to find shelter for the night. The spring wildflowers of orange, blue, red, yellow and purple carpeted both sides of the trail and as the sun dropped lower, began to close their blossoms. He would ride on for a time, he thought, hoping to find water and some good green grass for the General. The last golden beams of sunlight were disappearing when he found a good place to stop. There was a small creek with clean running water and lush green grass lined its banks, a perfect place to spend the night. Darkness had fallen when he pulled the saddle from Generals back and as he began to graze, he pulled some jerky from his saddle bags. As he ate he thought how wonderful it would be to again be with family sitting at a table covered with real food. A beef roast with potatoes and carrots and lots of gravy to soak up with fresh homemade bread had long been things of which he only dreamed. He checked the General and leaned back and placed his head on his saddle. Within minutes he was deep in sleep and with sleep came dreams of fighting and war.

The sun was just short of rising when he awoke and the General had his nose just above his face when he opened his eyes, so he reached up and gave him a good scratch between the ears. As he got to his feet he looked around and saw that the General had rested well for he could see where he had slept in the deep grass. He walked to the creek and washed his hands and face in the cool, clean water and then smoothed his long dark brown hair and pulled his hat down tight on his head. He picked up his saddle and blanket and placed it on the Generals back.

"Are you ready for another long ride?" he asked. "Let's get on home."

As he rode west he remembered the dreams of past night. As if they were exploding again, the brilliant reds and yellows of the cannon blasts were burned into his memory. The lush greens of the vegetation and trees on the battlefield gave way to fire from cannon and rifle fire, the result of which would take years to replenish. The charge forward toward the enemy was made even more difficult by the extreme number of dead and wounded soldiers lying helpless on the forest floor. Both blue and grey had suffered severe losses in the last battle of which he and the General had been a part. How many lives had been lost because of poor communication and how many battles had been fought after the signing of surrender he wondered? Memories were something he wished he could forget but knew they would be with him until he died.

From behind him he could hear the approach of what he thought would be a stagecoach. As it got closer, he moved the General to the side of the trail to allow it to pass. It was pulled by a six hitch of horses and the driver, a man of middle age with a thick brown beard, was yelling for the horses to pull harder for the slight grade that was just ahead. The man riding shotgun was another matter. As they drove by his eyes never left Josh and the shotgun he carried was aimed in his direction. The General moved a couple of steps back from the trail and when the coach had passed stepped forward and moved out as if to follow.

How he wished the stage had stopped so he could have had someone with whom to talk. His path had seen few travelers and most of them had been in a hurry or untrusting of strangers. The thought of home and friends was what kept him going and he knew that soon he would have plenty of both.

As he crested the rise in the trail he could see the stagecoach stopped at a creek not far ahead of him. He picked up the Generals pace with a slight gig of his spur. As he got closer to the coach he could see the shotgun rider closely watching his approach. "Who are you and what is your business?" the shotgun called out as he approached.

"Joshua Tidwell," he replied, "and I'm on my way home from the war."

The shotgun rider seemed to accept his explanation but still had a worried look in his eye. He wore a wide brimmed hat that shaded his entire face, a buckskin shirt and pants and boots the likes of which he had never seen before. They had laces which he had seen, but loud colored cloth sides which he hadn't. His face upon closer inspection betrayed the worry and uncertainty he felt about the approaching soldier.

"Stop to rest and water the stock?" Josh asked.

"Nope. We busted a wheel when the driver hit a rock in the creek," the shotgun rider answered.

"Anything I can do to help?"

"We can always use help," the driver answered as he came around to the back of the coach. "Did I hear you say you were a Tidwell? Not one of the Jason Tidwell's from down around Fort Worth."

"No, sir. I'm one of the Liam Tidwell's from Lincoln County, New Mexico Territory."

"Nice to meet you, son. And thanks for the offer to help," the driver added. "I'm Jamie Coulter and this cantankerous cuss is my shotgun rider Buckskin Jones. Everyone just calls him Buck. Let's get to work, huh."

Mr. Coulter, Josh could see, was older than he had originally thought, but was still agile for his age and ready to get the wheel of the coach repaired. His dark blue shirt was covered with dust and in places mud from sweat. His stature was buckled in the center perhaps from an accident involving his back, but his shoulders and arms betrayed the fact that he had long been wrestling with the reins of multiple hitch horses. When he brushed his thick brown beard with his hand, the dust flew.

"Josh, I'll get the horses. You get the singletrees. We'll use the whippletree to raise the back of the coach," Mr. Coulter called out. "Buck, you make sure we don't get any unwanted visitors."

As they worked they talked about the fix they were in. Buck said that since the end of the war, the roads were thick with outlaws and renegade soldiers just looking for people in a fix like they were in to plunder and kill at will. He said he was really glad they had no passengers when the wheel broke. But what they would be carrying after the next town stop was another matter.

Josh thought about what Buck had said about the road being dangerous for it hadn't seemed so to him. He had seen few travelers on the trail and guessed Buck was keeping himself sharp by believing at any time they might be set upon. Those on the trail that did choose to talk were more in a hurry than afraid of what they might encounter. Maybe he had just been fortunate and not been the target of thieves or renegades.

The wheel was replaced much faster than Josh had expected and the General seemed glad he and Josh were back on the road together. Both Jamie Coulter and Buckskin Jones waved as the coach rolled away and Josh somehow knew that their paths would someday cross again. He lightly spurred the General and once again they were heading west toward home.

While they worked on the coach wheel, Josh had asked where they were and how far it was to the next town and Buck had answered they were in Arkansas and the next town was Little Rock, about thirty miles farther to the southwest. "Just stay on the road and you can't miss it," Buck said with a bit of laughter in his voice. "Four years in the war, you're still alive, and you're lost. How'd you ever make it so long, son?" Buck laughingly joked.

Jamie Coulter agreed with a laugh and said, "Sure hope your folks ain't expectin' ya too soon."

Josh smiled as he rode through the pines of deep green and the thick grass the heat of the year was trying to turn from green to brown. Tomorrow he would be in Little Rock and he thought he might rest there for awhile for his travels so far had taken him from the bloody battlefields of Virginia, through the northwest portion of North Carolina and into Tennessee. He had crossed Tennessee and rode on into Arkansas and now he was only thirty miles from Little Rock. He still had half of Arkansas, Texas, and half of New Mexico to go to get home. Why did there have to be a Texas? It is in itself was one-third of his journey.

Little Rock was a bustling city that had joined the Confederacy in 1861. The Union Army took up residence there in 1863 and had a foot on the neck of the city maintaining Union authority even after the war ended. Josh had been warned of these events by Buck and thought he would give up his grey calvary uniform before entering Little Rock.

Mark Widmires traveling store afforded Josh a new suit of clothes and a wide brimmed felt hat that would keep the sun from his face.

Two conestoga wagons and two two horse hitches were the means of transport and all the goods a family could need were contained in those wagons. A light blue shirt, dark pants and a black hat replaced the confederate grey of a southern soldier. Josh was glad that he hadn't spent all of his pay unwisely for he found that he had enough for a new saddle for the General. He thought of the northern major that had contributed so generously to the purchase of the saddle. A musket ball just above the heart had taken his life and Josh knew he would have no further use for the money. It was the fortunes of war where the living prosper and the dead have had the honor of dying for their country. Mr. Widmire wrapped the clothing neatly in paper and tied it with some string. Josh took the package, thanked Mr. Widmire for stopping and rode off. He would find a good, clean creek to bathe in before he donned his new clothes.

The new saddle seemed to ride well on Generals back and there didn't seem to be a need for a harsh break in period. There were no unusual twitches or bowing of the back, so Josh felt the saddle was a good match to General. The twenty dollars he got for his old military saddle was just money in his pocket, money he would probably need in Little Rock.

Josh rode on to the west and when he thought he was ten or fifteen miles from the city, he found a place suitable for spending the night and for a bath in the morning. The saddle hadn't yet been removed from the Generals back when his nose dove into the thick, lush green grass that bordered the creek.

"Hungry, are you boy?" Josh said as he dropped the saddle to the ground. The General looked up just long enough for acknowledgement and then stuck his nose right back in the grass.

Josh went over the list of things he must do tomorrow in his mind. First, in the morning he would roll his uniform in his bedroll to keep it from being seen. Second, upon reaching town he would look for a barber shop and a place for a hot bath. Third, well third would take care of itself. Whatever came up, he would take it in stride and not make any trouble. Fourth was left for tomorrow for at three his head was on the new saddle, his eyes were shut, he was asleep. The General looked up from the grass to make sure all was well and then went back to eating.

The new clothes fit amazingly well, but the water of the creek had been especially cold. Josh had taken a quick bath and now stood dressed and ready to face the new day. He looked at himself in the clear blue water of the creek and decided from his reflection that he looked okay. He slowly turned around and took in the sights of tall green pines, lush green grass, and the purest blue of a cloudless spring sky. He saw the wildflowers open their petals to the first rays of the sun. He also remembered that the pines of Arkansas and eastern Texas would soon give way to the endless prairies of central and western Texas. That's probably why he took a few extra moments to enjoy the present scenery. He saddled General and then rode off. Little Rock was his next stop.

Little Rock was a beehive of activity and Josh thought he must have arrived on market day. As far as cities go, it was just like every other town in the south with a courthouse, churches, businesses and, of course, saloons. But it was the barber pole that most captured his attention. He tied General to the hitching rail and stepped up on the wooden boardwalk. He paused and turned to look up and down the main street. It was evident the Union Army was still a major player in the town. Union uniforms could be seen up and down the main street, in the businesses, and in the saloons. He turned and walked into the barber shop.

"Good morning, sir. Great day isn't it? Need a haircut and shave, do ya?" The barbers greeting was given with a smile that allowed everyone to know he was really glad to see you.

"Yep, I do," Josh replied. "You have a bath here?"

"Nope. The only bath house is in the hotel at the far end of the street," the barber said. "Climb up here in this chair and we'll see what we can do for you."

As Josh sat in the chair he asked, "You always have this many soldiers in town?"

"Most always. Some days there's a lot and other days there's just a few. No one knows why the number of 'em varies, but it does," was the barbers reply. "You wanna be careful around 'em 'cause most of 'em don't like bein' here and they're just plain mean. They know the wars over and they just wanna go home."

As they spoke, Josh watched what seemed to be endless amounts of dark brown hair fall from his head to his shoulders and to the floor. He wondered if his new hat would still fit.

Josh got out of the chair as the barber finished his cut, turned and looked into the large mirror hanging on the wall. He could actually see his ears again. He moved his head from side to side and said, "You did good. Thank you." He took a dollar coin from his pocket and flipped it to the barber.

"Let me get your change, sir."

"Keep it. You earned it long as my hair was," Josh replied. "Think I'll head up the street for that bath now. Thanks again."

The hotel surely wasn't the best in town but it was named the Fairmont and hopefully the bath water was hot. There was a small sign in the lobby of the hotel that read 'Best Bath House In Town' to which some drunk soldier or cowboy had added 'Only Bath House In Town'. The water was hot and there was plenty of it and the towels were soft and plentiful. So far Josh was really impressed with Little Rock.

General stood quietly at the hitching rail in front of the hotel. As Josh walked out his ears came forward and he was attentive to the wishes of his owner. Josh reached for the reins he had tied to the rail, but they were lying on the ground. Probably out of boredom, General had untied himself but he stood patiently waiting for Josh to return. The livery, Josh remembered, was at the opposite end of the street, so together he and General walked through town. As they made their way to the livery, Josh watched the ladies bustling from store to store purchasing the following weeks supplies. Dress shops, dry good stores, and hardware stores were all busy filling the needs of the residents that lived in the surrounding area. Most of the men were gathering at the gun shops, the blacksmith and saloons while the wives and children did the shopping. The stores were a variety of sizes. Some were large, like the mercantile while others were small as were the gun shop and the barber shop. Some of the buildings were recently constructed while it was evident others had been in place for years. All seemed freshly painted which gave one a sense that city pride was felt by all residents. Josh tipped his hat to those that glanced his way as he walked down the main street. It was a good looking young lady he was watching walk down the street that almost got him run over. General grunted and pulled to the right pulling Josh with him. It was the driver of the freight wagon that yelled, "Watch where you're goin', son. You're goin' ta git your butt run down."

Josh tipped his hat to the driver and said, "Sorry, sir."

The young lady he had been watching smiled, shook her head, and continued down the street. The blue and white dress she wore made it easy to find her in the crowd. Her blond hair fell softly around her flawless face but disappeared beneath the white parasol as she quickly turned and disappeared into a dress shop.

At the livery, Josh ordered a large stall, oats, and all the hay General wanted to eat. Once in the stall, he laid down in the fresh straw and began to roll. Josh spoke and the horse returned to its feet awaiting his next command, but it didn't come. Josh just gave him a good rub and then walked out of the livery. As he left he said, "Give him a good brushing and make sure he has plenty of fresh water."

The Bell Hotel was just up the street from the livery stable and Josh decided this would be the place he would spend the night. A real bed, a good hot meal, a drink and some friendly talk would be just what the doctor ordered. He registered at the hotel desk, got his room key and took his bed roll and saddle bags up to his room. He opened the curtains to let in some light, pulled his Navy Colt from its holster and checked each chamber and then looked out the window. Three times more he pulled the Colt from the holster each time faster than the time before. He was ready, but for what he didn't know. For anything, he surmised, and walked to the door and out of his room.

The bar in the Bell Hotel was a large room with the bar to the left, a stage at the far center of the room with burgundy curtains and tables to the center and right of the room. Two semi private boxes to the left and right of the stage were elegantly decorated with colorful curtains and brightly colored fabric covered chairs and Josh thought they must be for the more affluent of the city. Four Union soldiers were standing at the far end of the bar and maybe a dozen locals were seated at the tables. Four men sat at a far right table and were engrossed with the cards in their hands hoping each had the winning poker hand.

Josh walked to the bar and waited for the bartender to see him.

"What can I git ya, friend? We got just about anything you want to drink." The bartender was a bald man, skinny, but seemed to be a friendly kind.

"A beer. I think I'll start with a beer." Josh smiled and took a coin from his pocket to pay for his drink. As he took his first swallow, he saw one of the Union soldiers look in his direction.

The soldier turned back to his friends and said something Josh couldn't hear and then all four soldiers looked at him. It was a sergeant doing the talking and three privates doing the listening.

Josh looked into the mirror behind the bar and could see that none of the bar patrons were paying any attention to his presence. That was good. If trouble started, it would come from the far end of the bar. As Josh finished his first mug of beer he glanced around the room again. He noticed a very large man looking in his direction. He must be the local blacksmith Josh thought, for if he wasn't, he had really missed his calling. The blacksmiths glance left Josh and stopped at the four soldiers still drinking at the end of the bar. One of the privates dropped his mug of beer on the bar and walked toward Josh. He was the biggest of the three privates, but not as tall as Josh and Josh was no small man. He was just over six feet tall and his stature was that of a ranch hand, kind of wide at the shoulders and narrow at the waist. At around 190 pounds one could see that Josh could take care of himself.

As he walked ever closer, the private asked, "New around here aren't ya? I've not seen ya here before."

"Just passin' through," Josh replied.

"We don't take to strangers here about," the private said with a sneer in his voice.

"Just passin' through," Josh said again.

The sergeant saw that the private wasn't getting the reaction he wanted and told the private to check the identity papers Josh should be carrying.

"Let's have 'em, boy," the private said with a scowl.

"I'm just havin' a beer and minding my own business an' I suggest ya do the same." Josh was aware the sergeant was out to make trouble and though his feelings told him to be ready for anything, he maintained his composure and said in a low, soft voice "I think ya better git back ta yer beer."

"Are you telling me what to do? Guess you don't know we're the law around here?" The private moved ever closer. "I'll have yer papers or I'll have a piece of yer hide." He reached out to grab Josh by the shirt collar and in a flash was laying on the floor. Josh hit the private with a right hand to the jaw and the private collapsed.

"Guess he wasn't ready for that," Josh said in a voice of authority.

The sergeant and remaining two privates Josh could see were reaching for their guns. He hadn't wanted this, but would not back down from a good fight. He had had his fill of Union soldiers during the war and just because it was over wasn't about to bend to their will now. The sergeants gun was just clearing the holster when Josh went for his Navy Colt and in a flash he fired and the sergeant fell to the floor. The brilliant red and yellow flash from the Navy Colt flashed again as Josh dropped to the floor using the collapsed privates body for cover and fired the Colt twice more. The two privates fell where they stood without getting off a shot. Josh got to his feet and returned to his empty mug with his Colt still in his hand. The sound of a hammer being cocked caused him to fire once more. The third private lay dead on the floor.

The shooting had taken only seconds and four Union soldiers had been killed. This was nothing new for Josh. He had killed often during the war, but this shooting was senseless. Josh had bothered no one and four drunk soldiers had paid the ultimate price for their abuse of a stranger.

The blacksmith jumped to his feet as the last shot was fired. He rushed toward Josh and Josh brought his gun to bear on the large man.

"No friend. I'm here to help," he said as he walked. "Listen up ya'll. The law will be here shortly and everyone will have the same story. A man dressed in black burst through the door and shot the four soldiers. Got it." He looked around the room and saw that all were in agreement. "Let me have yer gun, son. We've gotta make sure ya have a way out of this before the law gits here." He took the Colt from Josh and placed it in the hand of the private on the floor. "He wanted to see yer gun and ya let 'em. Got it."

The bartender took the mug from Josh and refilled it. "Be drinkin' yer beer when the law comes in and act surprised. Ya really don't know what happened here. Right?"

Josh nodded agreement and took a big mouthful of beer. It was then that the sheriff and his deputy with two Union soldiers came through the saloon door.

"All right. What the hell's goin' on here?" the sheriff shouted as he entered the bar. He was a big man and instantly one could tell he was used to having his way. His face was shadowed by the wide brimmed grey felt hat he wore and his dark black mustache seemed to remain motionless as he spoke. The star on his chest was his badge of honor and he seemed to carry it proudly. His guns were in his hands and the deputy carried a ten gauge shotgun. His eyes raced around the room, but settled on Josh. The sheriff walked toward Josh, his eyes surveying the stranger and watching for some act of aggression. "Who are ya, son, and what the hell's goin' on here?"

Josh started to answer when the blacksmith interrupted and said, "He didn't have nothin' to do with it, Roy. Some guy dressed in black busted through the back door over there and started shootin'. The boy couldn't have done nothin' 'cause he didn't even have his gun. The private there on the floor asked to see his Colt and the man let 'im."

"That true, son. Is that what happened here?" the sheriff questioned.

"Yes sir. That's just what happened as I saw it. Who was that shooter anyway?" Josh asked.

"I don't know yet, but I will. This kind of thing doesn't happen in my town," the sheriff boasted. "Which way did he go, Tom? I didn't see nothing strange out front."

"Same way he came in, Roy. In and out through the same back door," the blacksmith, Tom, answered.

"We'll be after him then. Come on deputy. We got a murderer ta catch. You two soldiers git these bodies outta here and back ta the post." The sheriff and his deputy rushed out the back door and Josh hoped the worst was over.

"You okay, son? You don't seem to rattled," Tom asked of Josh. "You didn't do nothin' wrong here. These Union soldiers are always causin' trouble and it's only a matter of time before they git what's comin' to 'em."

"Thank you for your help, sir. I really appreciate it," Josh said. "I was goin' to stay the night, but I better git outta town quick. I'm on my way home and don't want to spend a lotta time here."

"Your leavin' in such a hurry is just gonna make the sheriff suspicious. I wouldn't leave 'til tomorrow if I was you. The sheriff seein' ya here will let him know you had no part of todays happenin'. My names Tom Rielly and I'm the town blacksmith."

Josh smiled and extended his hand to the man that had kept him from having to face a bunch of problems. He was introduced to the other patrons in the bar and each assured him their story of what had happened would not change. It was late when he finally made it to his room to sleep. He felt guilty for not going to the livery to check on General, but knew the horse would not hold it against him.

The sun was up when Josh awoke and he wondered how he could have overslept. This was something that just didn't happen. Maybe it was because he was really tired and the bed was so comfortable, but on the other hand, maybe he slept so well because of the numerous beers he had had the night before. He smiled as he thought of the men he had met last evening and how he had really enjoyed their company. It was, however, a shame that they had met under such circumstances. He dressed, washed up, grabbed his bed roll and saddle bags and walked out the door.

After a breakfast consisting of steak and eggs and lots of coffee, Josh walked out onto the main street boardwalk. It was evident that this day was no market day for few people were on the street and the blue coats of the Union soldiers were not to be seen. The good looking blond who yesterday had been dressed in blue and white this day wore light yellow and sat quietly in front of the stage depot. Her luggage was at her side. As he walked toward the livery he wondered where she was going and who was she going to see? And why would she wear yellow at this time of year? Bugs. They'd probably think she was some sort of flower, a very pretty flower. These were questions that interested him, but he knew they would never be answered. As he passed, he tipped his hat to her and told her to have a nice day. As he walked up the boardwalk toward the livery stable he thought of the pretty blond and searched his mind for a picture of her face, but saw only the face of Bonnie Davis, a childhood friend.

Approaching the livery, Josh thought he saw someone he knew. It was Buck, the shotgun rider that worked with Jamie Coulter. As quickly as he had appeared, he disappeared into the livery and as Josh arrived, the stage rounded the corner of the livery with Jamie and Buck high up in the drivers seat. They waved and shouted down to Josh and then were gone heading for the stage depot.

The General was up and his ears forward as Josh approached his stall. His midnight black coat was well brushed and he seemed to Josh to be ready for another day of travel. As the saddle blanket was placed on his back, General knew that it was time to go and the new saddle seemed to sit better than it had the day before. Josh swung the stall gate wide open, turned to General, placed his foot in the stirrup and climbed aboard the big stud. A light touch of his spur and General headed for the door of the livery. He nodded his approval to the livery owner and proceeded out to the street. The six bits it had cost to stable the General had been money well spent. He turned west and started out of town.

As he passed the stage stopped in front of the depot, he noticed the good looking blond was boarding the coach, her luggage already tied to the top. Seeing Jamie come out of the depot, he paused to talk.

"Good morning, Mr. Coulter. Heading back east again today."

"No sir. Goin' on to the west. Next big stop will be Texarkana, Texas. We should make it there in four days if the passenger we're waitin' for ever gits here," Jamie said in an irritated tone. "I just hate waitin'. Knocks me clear off my schedule."

"Well, you'll probably pass me long before Texarkana. Who ya waitin' for?" Josh asked.

"Some lawman comin' in from the north tryin' ta git ta Fort Worth. Must carry a load a water 'cause this line don't hold for no one." Jamie turned his attention to the young blond and continued, "Might as well come on down, missy. Looks like we're gonna be here fer awhile."

Josh told the stage driver he would see him on down the road, tipped his hat again to the young blond, and started off on his westward trek. He smiled as he thought of the smile given him in return of his tipped hat and again he wondered where it was she was headed.

Little Rock slowly disappeared in the east and once again Josh and General would have to depend on each other for company.

Chapter Two
It's a Long Way to Texarkana

The sun was high overhead and Josh was happy he had chosen a wide brimmed hat when he purchased his new clothes from Mr. Widmires Traveling Store. It was hot and General had worked up a good lather so he looked for a shady place with water to rest and get away from the sun. His hat was a bit loose though due to the amount of hair the barber had removed from his head in Little Rock. The shade of a giant live oak tree and the cool water of a small creek provided the pair with just what they needed, rest and a refreshing drink.

A little over two hours had passed when Josh decided they should get back on the road. The sun hadn't cooled any and the heat of the early afternoon seemed to be getting worse. Josh was half asleep in the saddle when the sound of gun shots brought him back to reality. He searched the landscape hoping to find the source of the gun fire. On a ridge overlooking the meadow through which he passed was a group of five riders. He stopped the General and tried to identify the riders now approaching him. He dropped his hand to his side and felt the Navy Colt and removed the leather catch from the hammer. He was ready for whatever the men closing on him had in mind. He was relieved when he recognized the sheriff from Little Rock.

"Tidwell, isn't it? You seen anyone 'round here today?" the sheriff asked.

"No, sir. Y'all are the first people I've seen since leaving Little Rock. Did you pick up the trail of that shooter from yesterday?" Josh was certain the lawman didn't suspect him, so he decided to be as helpful as possible.

"Nope. Never picked up a trail. Seems he just vanished. Now we're on the trail of two Indians that killed a family of settlers a couple of miles back over that ridge." The sheriff pointed to the south. "Keep a sharp eye out for 'em, boy. They know when they're caught they're dead, so they got nothing to lose."

"That I'll do, sheriff. And thanks for the warning."

With that said the sheriff and his posse wheeled their horses to the east and rode back toward Little Rock. As he rode away the sheriff turned in his saddle and glanced back at the cowboy on the big black horse. Somehow he felt there was more to this man than he had been allowed to know. He shook his head realizing he would never know the truth, squared himself in his saddle and continued riding on to the east.

The road was unending to the west and he couldn't remember if it was one or two stage relay stations he had passed. Hour after hour and day after day the General and Josh kept riding to the west realizing that sooner or later they would make it home. It was the third relay stop they came upon when Josh decided to call it a day. The shadows cast by the hills and the tall pines were growing long and the clouds were gathering to the northwest. It would soon rain and Josh wanted to find some dry cover for the night. The relay station attendant came out to meet them as they approached his home.

"Evenin' stranger. What can I do for ya?" the man asked. He was a stout man quite capable in size to change a hitch of horses in a short amount of time. His reddish brown hair was just short of shoulder length and seemed to be sticking straight out from beneath his straw hat. His overalls were dirty and his plaid shirt soaked with sweat. "Come on down and rest awhile."

Josh swung his leg over General and lowered himself to the ground. He extended his hand and the two men shook hands. As their hands met, Josh noticed the large silver ring on the attendants right hand. On the top of the ring was the letter B which he thought came from his name.

"Wonder if I can spend the night in yer barn? It's gonna be raining' shortly and I sure would like ta stay dry."

"Stay in the barn. Heck, the wife and kid are in Little Rock so ya can stay in the house. I'll be glad ta have some company. My name's Bill Smith," the relay station attendant said. "As far as it raining, hasn't rained here in a month."

"Josh Tidwell. Nice to meet you."

Josh settled General in the barn for the night and then walked toward the station, Bill chattering constantly at his side. They were about half way to the station house when they saw the first flash of lightning and then heard the first clap of thunder. Ten minutes after entering the station it began to pour.

The next morning Josh was up early and anxious to get back on the trail toward home. The rain of the previous night had washed the dust from the air and it now smelled fresh and clean. He went to the barn and gave General some fresh hay and water. As for himself, two cups of coffee and he was ready to get under way. Bill talked constantly as Josh saddled General and was still chattering as Josh rode away.

Josh was glad that he had the opportunity to let Bill know about the two renegade Indians the sheriff had told him about. No one could know where they would appear next or what havoc they might inflict on an innocent traveler. All Josh knew is that Bill was a grown man, and being so was responsible for his own wellbeing. He did suggest the station attendant wear a sidearm or keep a rifle within reach in case of an emergency. But Bill could probably talk them to death. He smiled at the thought and then began to laugh aloud.

As with every other day, the trail toward Texarkana, Texas was unending and as the hours passed the weather got hotter and hotter. Josh was half asleep in the saddle and missed the lush greens of the trees and shrubbery that lined the trail and the screech of the bald eagle flying high overhead. His horse, General, didn't miss the thick grass that was abundant on each side of the trail. He just wanted to stick his nose in the deep green grass and eat for awhile. And it was only General that had seen the five deer cross the road ahead of them. The does paid no attention to his approach, but the big buck, a ten pointer at least, paused briefly to look in their direction and then bound off into the woods. Later he saw pheasants take to the air to clear the path of the westward travelers.

General knew that Josh was still asleep for he sat motionless in the saddle. There was no jerking from side to side, a motion caused by countless hours in the saddle. An approaching wagon was the reason General bucked to bring his rider back to life.

The eastward bound wagon that shared the trail was filled with household goods and Josh knew that it was a family on the move. Two chairs, a small table and three trunks probably holding clothing and household goods and a small redheaded boy in bib overalls were in the back of the wagon. The boys parents sat in the front and their faces betrayed the fear they felt for having to leave their home. The man looked to be in his thirties and tired. The woman, perhaps two or three years younger seemed on edge and seemed to be unhappy about the fix they were in. They both stopped and exchanged greetings. Josh learned from the travelers that a Union Army patrol had been dispatched to warn all families in the area of the danger the two Indians were causing. "Must be the same two Sheriff Roy told him about," he thought. It was evident the family was in a hurry to reach safety for Josh saw the woman's arm appear from beneath her grey knitted shawl. She tugged on the sleeve of her husbands tan shirt letting him know she was ready to continue their journey. Josh wished them safe travel and they started again their eastward trip. Josh and General watched the wagon for a moment and then turned back to the west.

It seemed to Josh that the pair of Indians in question were covering a lot of ground to have burned a home just outside of Little Rock and now be raising cain more than half way to Texas. He had better keep a sharp eye out as the sheriff had suggested or he could end up one of their targets. He scanned the landscape as they continued west. The landscape seemed to disappear from view and a wartime mental attitude took over his thinking. All his senses were on the alert and he rode as if expecting an ambush. The ride now held his attention and the thick green forest and the multicolored wild flowers he passed were unseen for his mind was set on the Indians.

As the sun began to set, Josh turned off the trail and rode into a thick grove of tall pine trees. So thick was the ground vegetation that he didn't think he could be seen from the trail and he would maintain a cold camp for a fire might be visible to anyone passing by. He settled the General and walked over to a large rock, sat down and leaned back against it. He closed his eyes.

As he slept, he dreamed of battles in which he had participated and they brought about a restlessness he had only experienced since going to war. He was with his cavalry unit and they were charging a cannon emplacement when a cannonball struck a tree he was passing. The impact of the cannonball exploded the tree and a large splinter penetrated his right side. It felt as if he had been speared with a saber and he could feel the blood running down to his leg. He struggled to stay in the saddle and pulled the wood from his side. General stopped as he fell from his back and he stood guard until corpsmen found him and took him to a field hospital. It was later in the hospital he was told about the loss of over a third of his unit in that charge. The rest of the night his mind jumped from battle to battle and though he slept, he really got no rest and in the morning that followed his revisited battles, he felt as if he hadn't slept at all.

The first light of a beautiful morning found Josh and General again heading west. A slight morning breeze caused the pines to gracefully sway as if keeping time with the music of some country ballad. Squirrels and rabbits scurried around in the days early light. The squirrels gathered food and their cheeks were fat with the gains of their hunt. They stood erect to see what it was that distracted them from their hunt for food. The rabbits paid little attention to the horse and rider as they passed and continued to breakfast on the deep grass. A buzzard high atop a giant pine spread his wings flexing them in preparation for a long day of flight. And the two traveled on.

As he rode west, Josh felt as if someone was watching him. So strong was the feeling that he rode to a high knoll to the north for a better view of the terrain through which he passed. He saw nothing. He and General returned to the trail and continued to the west, but the feeling was still there. He knew that shortly someone would be crossing their path. If the Indians had watched him the day before, they would know that as the afternoon heated up Josh would sleep while still in the saddle. He decided he would act as if he were again sleeping to see what his actions might bring. He kept up his act for four or five miles and then decided he was worrying about something that wasn't going to occur. It was as he sat up in the saddle that he heard the sound of running hoofbeats come out of the trees to the right behind him and out of habit spurred the General and he began to run. Josh turned in the saddle to see what was behind him. It really didn't surprise him to see the two Indians that were creating so much havoc in the area closing in on him.

He had never fought Indians before and thought his Colt against their bows and arrows placed the odds strictly in his favor. The whistling of an arrow passing close to his left ear immediately changed his thinking. He pulled his Navy Colt from its holster and turned in the saddle. He fired once and missed as did his second shot. He had to position himself for a better line of fire, but what could he do? He thought of the best horse rider he had ever seen, an Indian, and decided to copy his style. He shoved his left boot to the heel in the stirrup, grabbed the horn tightly with his left hand and swung his right leg over General's back as if to dismount. Now he faced to the rear of the horse and was face to face with the Indians. Again he fired the Colt and the Indian to the left of the duo fell from his horse and the second stopped to help his friend. Josh pulled himself up and swung himself back to General's back and as he did wheeled the big black around to the right and he was after the second Indian. The remaining Indian pulled an arrow from his quill and drew his bow. As he did, Josh fired the Colt and as the Indian fell his arrow flew harmlessly into the woods.

Both Indians rode horses with rifles in the scabbards attached to the saddles and Josh wondered why they would use a bow and arrow rather than the rifle. It made no sense to him for their attack would have been much more frightening had they used the rifles. They had the advantage and let it slip away. Josh loaded the first Indian on his pinto, cut a strip of leather from his quill and tied his hands to his feet beneath the horses chest. He wanted proof that the threat to the area settlers was now over. As he lifted the second Indian to the back of his short sorrel he noticed the Indian's left hand. He wore a silver ring with the letter B engraved on it. It was the ring he had seen on Bill Smith's hand when he shook his hand at the stage relay station. Bill hadn't been able to talk them to death, but Josh knew he hadn't gone down without a fight. Josh removed the ring from the Indians finger and vowed he would send it to Bill's wife as soon as he reached Texarkana.

Josh tied the reins of the sorrel to the tail of the pinto and made sure both horses and Indians were ready for travel. The horses weren't Indian ponies for both were shod and their feet had been well cared for. The farrier who maintained their feet was an expert, for Josh could see the remains of a quarter crack in the cornet band of the sorrel's left front foot. General stood patiently and when Josh put his foot in the left stirrup to mount, he stood motionless. Josh circled General close to the pinto, leaned over and picked up the pinto's reins, checked to make sure the sorrel was securely tied to the pinto and then they were on their way. Next stop, Texarkana, Texas.

The sign said "Texarkana Town Limits - Population Unknown". He had finally arrived in Texas and Josh wanted to get rid of the Indians that followed him. As he rode into town, he saw a gathering of people in the street and the closer he rode, he could see the gathering was in front of the sheriff's office. As he rode closer yet, heads in the crowd turned in his direction and the sound of their voices became silent. It must have had something to do with the two bodies he had in tow.

It was the sheriff that approached him first.

"What 'cha got there, stranger? You got a heap of explainin' ta do ta git yerself clear of them two Indians," the sheriff said in a gruff voice. He was tall and skinny and Josh wondered how this man could demand any respect from the town folk. His clothes seemed freshly laundered and his boots were shiny and dustless. He wore his gun low on his left side and Josh believed it to be a pearl handled Colt Peacemaker. When he reached in his pocket to retrieve the ring he took from the dead Indians finger, he found out how this skinny sheriff got respect from the townspeople. Josh's hand had barely moved toward his pocket and the sheriff had his Colt pointed at his head. It had to be the fastest draw he had ever seen.

"You kill them Indians?" the sheriff asked again.

"I think they're the ones everybody's been looking for," Josh said and showed the ring to the sheriff. "This ring belonged to a relay station attendant over in Arkansas. I saw it on his hand just a couple of days ago and I took it from one of the Indians."

The sheriff was inspecting the Indians and looking for a brand on the horses. He too had noticed right off that the horses were shod, so they weren't Indian ponies, they belonged to a white man. As he continued his inspection he said, "what ya gonna do with the ring, son? It don't belong to you ya know."

"I'm sendin' it ta his wife in Little Rock. That's where she was when I stopped by the relay station couple of days back."

The sheriff continued to question Josh as if he were a suspect in a murder he'd known nothing about until Josh told him. He was a stranger in the town, but would he be so stupid to tell the sheriff about a murder he knew nothing about if he had committed it? Something was wrong here and it wasn't with Josh. This sheriff might be real fast on the draw, but there was no doubt he wasn't the sharpest tack in the pail.

His inspection of the horses and the Indians completed, he turned to address the crowd.

"Well, folks. Looks like this here young man has answered all yer questions about what them Indians are up ta and where they're raidin'. They ain't raidin' and they ain't up ta nothin'. They're right here deader than dirt."

After receiving thanks from the Texarkana towns people, Josh looked for the telegraph office for he wanted to let Sheriff Roy in Little Rock know that the Indians for which he searched had been killed just short of Texas. He also wanted someone to check on Bill Smith at the stage relay station.

Having sent his telegram, Josh returned to the street and headed for where he had tied General and it was then that the stagecoach rolled into town. He could tell right off that the driver was Jamie Coulter by the way he yelled at the horses and the buckskin dressed shotgun, Buckskin Jones. Josh wondered if the blond dressed in yellow would still be on board the coach. He would know shortly for the stage driver, Jamie, was yet to start to slow.

"Yo, Josh," Jamie called from the from his seat. "What ya up to here. Thought you'd be close ta home by now."

"Just as fast as I can, Mr. Coulter. Just as fast as I can." He looked toward Buck and touched the brim of his hat in a silent greeting for Jamie had yet to stop talking.

Josh had to know about the blond, so he walked to the side of the coach and looked in. She was just getting ready to exit the coach when Josh appeared so she extended her hand to him to help her from her seat.

"We keep seeing each other so I guess we might as well introduce ourselves," she said with a big smile. "I'm Melissa Ryon and I'm on my way home to Fort Worth. And you are?"

"Tidwell, ma'am. Joshua Tidwell and I'm on my way home to Lincoln County, New Mexico Territory. Most just call me Josh though." His smile was genuine and he had two of the answers to the questions he wanted to know about her in Little Rock. He knew her name and where she was going. Now, all he needed to know is who was she going to see?

Why was it that each time he thought of Melissa he saw Bonnie Davis's face? She was a real pest when they were young and couldn't figure out why she would appear in his minds eye now.

"Ya ought ta know, Missy, he's a good worker too. Helped me change a coach wheel the other side of Little Rock. Had that wheel changed in nothin' flat," the driver said as he climbed to the top of the coach. He untied the young woman's baggage and then motioned for Josh to get ready to take it from him.

"Listen up, Jamie. Ya know them Indians everyone was searchin' for over in Arkansas, the kid here killed 'em," Buck said as he came out of the stage depot. "Guess the kids got more than one talent, right? And that relay attendant, Bill, it was the Indians that killed 'im. The kid found his ring on one of their fingers."

"Is that right?" Melissa asked. "Is that really what happened?"

Josh nodded his head in affirmation. "It ain't nothin' ta be proud of, but yes, that's what happened." He wanted to stay and talk with her, but he had told the sheriff he would sign papers as to what actions he had taken on the trail and he had to go to his office.

As he started toward the sheriff's office he turned and asked Jamie, "What happened to that lawman you were waitin' for in Little Rock?"

"Never showed up, son. Guess he found some other way to Fort Worth."

Josh nodded his head, turned again and walked off to meet with the sheriff.

The sun had not reached its high point yet and it grew hotter by the minute and Josh thought how good it was going to be to once again be in the high mountains of Lincoln County. It would still be cool there and the high temperature of the day wouldn't be as hot as it already was in Texarkana.

"Got the papers ready fer ya, son. Just write down what ya did and why ya did it and we'll be done," the sheriff said as he reached for his cup of coffee. "Have some?" He held an empty cup out for Josh.

"Nope. It's to hot for coffee. But a nice cool beer would sure go down good right now." Josh sat down at the desk and looked at the papers in front of him.

"You can read and write, can't ya? If not, I'll give you a hand in just a minute." The sheriff walked over to a wooden box at the far side of the room, opened the door and pulled out a beer. "If ya haven't seen one before, it's called an ice box and it keeps the beer pretty cold." He handed the beer to Josh.

"I can read and I can write and you can be sure that what I write is just what happened." The question about Josh's literacy didn't bother him. Most people just made their mark when signing papers. Schools were few and far between in most areas and children were needed at home to help with the farms or ranches of their parents.

"What ya gonna do with them horses, son? They ain't got no brands so we got no way ta tell who they belonged to. Ya gonna take 'em with ya?" the sheriff asked.

"I guess they would be mine 'cause I found 'em, but I don't want that sorrel. He's too small. I'll take the pinto with me and as far as I'm concerned, you can have the sorrel."

Josh finished with the paperwork, swallowed the last few drops of his beer and got up to leave.

"Ya did the town a big favor killin' them Indians, son. The town thanks ya and I thank ya. Maybe now the town'll settle down and git back to normal, 'cause they sure been stirred up since hearin' 'bout them Indians." The sheriff extended his hand to Josh. "I thank ya 'cause now I don't have to go out and hunt for 'em." He smiled a big smile as Josh turned and exited the office.

Josh walked back to the hitching post where he had left General. He loosened the sorrel's reins from the pinto's tail and led the sorrel back to the sheriff's office. The sheriff nodded his approval as Josh tied the horse to a porch roof support. They didn't speak again, but each of them knew that Josh had made the sheriff's job a lot easier.

General waited patiently for Josh's return, but kicked every so often at a fly that buzzed around beneath him. As Josh walked back to the big stud, he swatted at a bee that had landed on his left shirt sleeve. As he swatted, dust flew and he realized it was time for another bath and some clean clothes. He untied both the General and the pinto from the hitching post and led them to the livery stable.

"Time for you two ta get some rest and a good meal. Some oats might go real good 'bout now, huh boy?" Josh talked to his horse all the time, sometimes from boredom and others as quick commands because of impending danger. He knew General understood the words he spoke for they had been together since the horse had been foaled. He again swatted at the pesky bee and again the dust flew. He was going to have to wear his duster whether it was hot or not, but a bath and clean clothes were a must.

His horses set for the night, Josh walked back toward the stage depot. The stage was still in front of the depot and he thought he might see the pretty Melissa Ryon again. He opened the door and walked into the building.

"Hey, Josh. The sheriff didn't lock up the big Indian killer?" Jamie asked while scratching his thick brown beard and trying to keep from laughing. "Me and Buck was bettin' on if we'd see ya again or not." With that said, both he and Buck could no longer hold back the laughter.

"Real funny, boys. Real funny," Josh replied. "Where's Melissa?" he asked.

"Gone, son. She left on the stage 'bout fifteen minutes ago."

"You joshin' me. I'm not blind and I can see the stage sittin' out front."

"She left on the other stage, the spare they keep here. Guess they needed it for the run from Fort Worth west and rather than rollin' an empty stage, they just swapped 'em. Anyway, the station attendant here found a dry wheel on our coach and it'll take 'em a while to grease 'em all. Guess me and Buck'll be layin' over here for a spell. Ya know, this run only runs once a week."

"You two always bring the stage this far?" Josh asked as he sat in an empty chair.

"No, sir. We asked fer a transfer and got it. We'll probably be sittin' atop that stage that just left here in a couple of weeks. That's why we come this far."

"What about yer families?" Josh questioned. "They gonna join up with ya in Fort Worth?"

"Family? Ain't got no family. Buck's the closest thing I got ta family and there's times I don't claim him." Jamie looked toward Buck and smiled.

Buck just leaned back in his chair and sneered back at Jamie.

One could tell in a short time that these two men were the best of friends. The three men talked for a while and Josh learned much about the two friends that shared a lot more than the drivers seat of a stagecoach.

It was when the depot attendant entered the room from the street that Josh got up to leave. He was almost to the door when he remembered the ring in his pocket. He turned back and walked toward the attendant.

"Something I can do for you, sir? I'll be happy to help in any way I can," the station attendant said. He was a small man, bald with a short ring of hair from ear to ear around the back of his head. He wore a visor to shade his eyes, black trousers, a white shirt with two arm bands just above the elbows and a black vest. One could immediately see this man was proud of his position and thought of nothing but business. There was something about him that let Josh know he had few friends for his bearing was dry and all that mattered to him was his office and the stage line.

"I have a ring here that belonged to one of yer company's employees. His name was Bill Smith and he ran a relay station over in Arkansas. I wonder if ya could send it back to Little Rock and make sure it gits to his wife." Josh held out the silver ring so the attendant could see it.

The attendant said nothing, but reached behind the counter and came out with an envelop.

"Put her name and the city on the outside of the envelop, place the ring in the envelop and then seal it. I will make sure it gets on the next stage east. It leaves tomorrow at seven o'clock in the morning."

Josh was now sure that his initial impression of the man was correct. This man was all business and dry as a desert dried bone.

"He was a good man," Buck injected. "We found him just as the Indians left him. He was split top to bottom. Not something ya really wanna see every day. Just glad his wife hadn't been a passenger on that trip."

Josh handed the envelop to the attendant and turned toward the door. He nodded to Buck and Jamie and walked out the door. The street was empty as Josh stepped out of the depot. The high heat was what probably kept the residents in their homes and businesses. He walked across the street and into the Paris Hotel. He got a room and stuck the room key in his pocket. The emporium for clean clothes, the bathhouse for a bath, and having donned his clean clothes walked to the laundry. His dirty clothes would be ready in the morning the old woman that ran the laundry told him.

He now wore a tan shirt, brown vest, grey trousers and his Navy Colt. A good brushing of his black felt hat had made it look as good as new. He returned to the hotel and walked into the dining room where he found Buck and Jamie eating an early dinner. Seeing him enter the room, they motioned for him to come over and join them. The pork roast, boiled potatoes, string beans and coffee were just what his body had needed. And the gravy, it was almost as good as his mother had made when he was still at home.

The three friends made it from the dining room to the bar and after a few drinks, Josh excused himself and made his way to his room.

"Good morning, sir. Nice day, isn't it?"

"Ellie, don't bother the man," the young girl's mother snapped.

"No bother, ma'am. And yes, it is a beautiful day, young lady." Josh thought the little girl was really a cute little thing, but he could see she was in trouble for talking to a stranger.

As Josh walked down the street toward the livery stable he saw the east bound stage in front of the depot. As the passengers boarded the coach he saw the depot attendant hand the shotgun rider a mail bag and then the envelop containing Bill Smith's ring. At least the dry old man was a man of his word, Josh thought. He hoped receiving the ring would help Bill's wife and son feel better.

General and the pinto had been well cared for and their coats had received a good brushing. Their noses were still deep in the hay they had been given earlier in the morning. The sound of Josh's voice brought General's head up and his ears forward and he knew they would soon leave and continue their journey to the west. Josh entered General's stall with his saddle and blanket and as he placed them on his back, thought of the pinto. He didn't know the pinto's name. That was okay. He'd give the horse a new name, but he'd have to think about it. It took time to find the right name for General and he'd do the same for the pinto. After saddling his stud, he entered the pinto's stall and put on the halter and lead rope he had purchased at the feed and seed store. He led the two from their stalls and out to the street, stuck his foot in the stirrup and settled himself in the saddle. After stopping at the hotel for his bed roll and saddle bags and the laundry for his clean clothes, he and his horses were on their way west again. Sulphur Springs would be his next city stop.

Chapter Three
Next Stop, Sulphur Springs

As the trail had been from Little Rock to Texarkana, so it was now as Josh headed on to the west and to Sulphur Springs. Long, hot, and endless was the trail and his journey. The only real change he could see was that the tall pines were giving way to more and more cedars with a few live oaks and red oaks thrown into the landscape. He was nearing the wide open prairie expanse where buffalo had once roamed freely and where one could see for miles. It was now mid June and the evening air had not yet started to cool. Josh thought at this time of year he should be needing to wear his duster to keep him comfortably warm, but the weather was like that of late July or August. As he rode he thought of his new rifle.

Josh had never felt comfortable using a rifle. He felt his Colt was all he needed, but seeing a new Henry rifle in the gun shop in Texarkana had perked his interest. As he rode, he reached down and pulled the Henry from the new case he had attached to the right side of his saddle, wrapped the reins around the saddle horn to free both his hands and brought the Henry up to his shoulder. It felt better than what he expected, but it did cause him to have to carry two different calibers of ammunition. The Navy Colt was a thirty-six caliber and the Henry a forty-four caliber rim fire. As much as he hated the thought of no longer carrying the Navy Colt, he might have to change to a hand gun that used the same ammunition as his new rifle.

He liked the lever action and used it to chamber a bullet. He took careful aim at the branch of a tree and fired. He missed, but the crack of the rifle set the pinto to bucking and pulling back on the saddle where Josh had attached the lead rope. The pinto reared and jumped from the left side of General to the right and as she did knocked Josh from the saddle to the ground. General stopped and stood motionless and waited for Josh to pick himself up and climb back into the saddle. The rifles report was nothing new to General for he had carried Josh through many battles. The pinto, however, was still bucking and Josh had to quiet the horse by giving her a good rub. Josh knew he wouldn't try that again.

With everything back to normal, Josh moved General and the pinto onward and thought how he would have to get the multicolored horse accustomed to gun fire. Later in the day he would stop, tie the pinto to a tree, and then fire a few shots from close to where the pinto would stand. If he repeated this process each day, he believed the mare would soon pay no attention to gun fire. He stood up in the stirrups and rubbed his backside where it had hit the ground. Butt Spot, Josh thought. That's what he should name the pinto. The horse was spotted and had been the cause of a sore butt, so the name was more than appropriate. He smiled and thought no, he couldn't do that to a nice horse.

The wind began to blow and the dust began to fly. Josh pulled his handkerchief from his pocket and tied it over his nose and mouth. He dropped his head to allow the wide brim of his hat to keep the dust from his eyes. As he did, he noticed the pinto's mane. It was long and bright white and waved wildly in the breeze.

"I've got it. I'll name you Windy. That's a good name for a pinto mare. Yes, that's what it will be from now on." Looking at the mare he said, "from now on, you're Windy."

The threesome had been on the trail for about six hours and Josh was wondering how Windy would ride, so he stopped under a huge live oak and swapped the saddle and bridal from General to Windy. He would ride her until he decided to stop for the night. As he climbed into the saddle and returned to the trail, he found her gait to be smooth and she worked well using leg commands. He had definitely chosen the right horse. The saddle that had come with Windy was old and worn and Josh had sold it and the carbine rifle to the sheriff. General didn't seem to mind the change and the three would go farther each day by using both horses to carry his weight.

Josh began to think about the results of his firing of the new Henry. Windy was probably half asleep when he had shot at the tree limb and if he had made sure she was aware of what was going on, she probably would have been okay. He reached for the rifle, then paused. No, he thought, I'll wait 'til later in the trip to try that again.

Josh knew they had to be close to a relay station and thought he might spend the night there. Someone to talk to other than a horse would be a delightful change. Hot food instead of jerky was also on his mind. He looked carefully at the land before him, but could see no sign of the station so he kept on riding. It was as he reached the top of a small rise that he could see the smoke from the relay stations stove in the valley below. He lightly spurred the mare and she picked up a trot. He had been in the saddle all day and he was ready to rest. The trot would get him there just a little faster.

As Josh got closer to the relay station he could see that the smoke he had seen was getting heavier and as the station came into view could see the smoke came from the barn. It was on fire. As he closed on the barn, he saw a man lying on the ground motionless. He quickly dismounted and ran to the injured man and checked his wounds. He had been shot just below the right shoulder and Josh hoped it hadn't penetrated his lung.

He wasn't having much luck at stopping at relay stations. First there was Bill Smith and now this man. As he was checking for other wounds, the man regained consciousness and started to speak.

"Check on my wife," he whispered. "Find out if my wife's okay. Her name's Martha."

Josh ran to the house and burst through the door. "Martha," he called. "Martha, I'm here to help. Where are you?" He went into the bedroom. Not there. He started for the back door and then paused thinking he heard something in the kitchen. As he walked into the kitchen area he heard it again, a soft knock from beneath a trap door in the floor. Josh pulled the door open and found himself looking down the double barrels of a shotgun.

"Easy with that thing, ma'am. I'm here to help and we have to git back to yer husband. He's been shot." He extended his hand to help her back to the floor of the kitchen and then both hurried back to where her husband lay on the ground.

Martha checked her husbands wound and said, "We've got to get him to a doctor. You get the wagon and harness up the mare and I'll try to stop the bleeding."

As Josh ran toward what was left of the barn, he could see the stage horses had been run out of the coral and they were lucky the horse thieves had overlooked the mare still in the stall in the barn. He grabbed a burlap bag as he entered the barn and then a halter and lead rope. The mare was moving from side to side of her stall and Josh threw the lead rope around her neck to quiet her. He wrapped the burlap bag around her head and then pulled the halter on over it to hold the bag in place. He threw open the stall door and quickly led the mare away from the fire and out of the barn to safety.

Martha called to Josh as he and the mare exited the burning barn. "Harness is in the tack room behind the house."

Josh nodded and led the horse to the tack room. As he harnessed the mare to the wagon, he saw Martha for the first time. She was old beyond her years and her grey flannel dress was far from new. She wore a white apron that had seen better days and her shoes were well worn boots. Josh climbed aboard the wagon and drove to where Martha patiently waited. As the two loaded the wounded man in the back of the wagon, Martha began to speak. Tears filled her eyes and she brushed her grey hair away from her face with a bloody hand.

"My husband's name is Ben. Ben Robinson. We been out here

nearly five years and nothin' like this ever happened before. It was horse thieves that shot my man. Horse thieves."

Martha said the nearest doctor was in Mount Pleasant, about twelve miles to the west. Josh hoped her husband would make it that far.

Josh tied General and Windy to the back of the wagon and then climbed into the drivers seat. Martha sat in the back with her husband, his head cradled in her lap. As he drove, he looked back at Ben. His white shirt was well worn around the collar and cuffs and now covered with blood. He seemed to be younger than Martha, but not by much. He was still in good shape for his age and his big hands told a story of a life of hard work. Martha held her husband's brown, worn hat in her right hand and kept it in a position that shaded his face from the afternoon sun. It seemed to take forever to cover those twelve miles to the doctor and when the town came into view, Martha, who had remained quiet the entire ride, said the doctor's house was the first you came to on the left. As they stopped in front of the home, Josh saw a sign that read Dr. Sam Wilton, M.D. A young woman came out and helped them get Ben into the house.

Josh waited outside the house for someone to let him know how Ben was doing. The sun had long set and darkness was upon him and it seemed hours had gone by before Martha came out.

"He's going to be fine. The doc said the bullet missed his lung and he'll be real sore for a bit, but he'll be fine. I want to thank you for your help, but I don't even know your name," the old woman said. "The doc sent his son to git the marshall and the stage station master. They'll take care of things back at the house."

"Joshua Tidwell, ma'am. But most just call me Josh. Glad I could help. You gonna be okay, ma'am? If so, I think I'll find somewhere to spend the night."

Martha took his hand and said, "I'll be fine. I'm stayin' here with Ben. Bless you for savin' my husband's life. I'll never forget you."

Josh smiled, tipped his hat and walked to the wagon where his horses were still tied. He climbed aboard Windy and, with General in tow, rode off into the dark to find food, a livery stable and a hotel. There was room for the horses at the stable, but the hotel was full and Josh spent the night above his horses in the hay loft.

It was early in the morning that Josh was awakened by the sound of someone moving around below. He thought it was probably the hired help in to feed the animals. Josh got up and walked to the edge of the loft and watched the man below. He was talking to the horses as he fed them fresh hay.

"Morning," Josh said.

The man below jerked around in a surprised manner and said, "Gees mister. You scared the beejesus outta me. I didn't know ya were up there."

"Sorry 'bout that. Ya gotta place a man can wash up around here?"

"In the back. There's a basin and fresh water in the barrel. This black and pinto your horses? They're really good stock."

Josh nodded in affirmation and walked to the back to clean up.

"You hear about Ben Robinson? He got shot and the horses at the relay station was stolen."

"Yep. I'm the one that brought 'em to the doc. How'd ya hear 'bout it?"

"It's all over town already."

"Where's the best place in town to eat? I'm starvin"

"Millies Place. Only place open in town at this hour."

"I'll be back for the horses after I git some food in my stomach. Won't be long, I wanna git on the road."

It was too early for there to be much foot traffic on the street and Josh took his time walking up the boardwalk to the restaurant and took in the sights of the main street in town. There were dress shops, a hardware store, a gun shop and an emporium and he hadn't gone a quarter of the way up the street. This town must be pretty prosperous to have so many businesses, he thought. He passed a small park area with closely mowed grass, two giant and very old live oaks and a well. It must have been the community well from which the business owners drew the water, he thought. The businesses were painted in various colors. The emporium was white, which was the predominant color, but the gun shop was a tan color and the barber shop a light blue. Some roofs were wood shake while others were covered in metal, probably tin, he thought. He walked on to Millie's.

Millie's Place did have the best food in town or was it that he was just so hungry? The only words he spoke while in the restaurant were those he spoke to order his food. Must be too early for conversation, he thought. He finished his bacon and eggs, six biscuits with jam and three cups of coffee, paid the bill and walked out the door without having said another word or having anyone speak to him. There wasn't even a have a nice day said as he left.

As he walked back to the livery he noticed a few of the shop owners were opening their stores, but Josh didn't enter any. This wasn't to friendly a town so early in the morning and he hated to be ignored. To bad he wouldn't be here later in the day to see if the conversation loosened up or not. The man at the livery had said word was all over town 'bout Ben, but if they didn't talk to each other, how had the word spread?

Josh saw a well dressed man standing in front of the livery with a shotgun held across his chest as he neared the stable. What was going on now he wondered as he walked on.

"You the one that helped the Robinson's yesterday?" he asked as Josh entered the livery.

"Yep," was his answer. It was then that he saw the star on his chest and in the middle was written deputy.

"I wanted to thank ya for what ya did, friend. They's kin, my aunt and uncle."

"How's Ben doin'?" Josh asked as he jokingly thought that people in this town really do talk.

"Fine, sir. I've told 'em a hundred times they's to old to be workin' that relay by themselves. Fact is, I been tryin' to get 'em ta move inta town and live with me. Hard as Uncle Ben's worked all his life it's about time fer him to take a rest by retirin'. Maybe this'll be enough to change their minds and they'll make the move."

"Ol' Ben doesn't seem the type ta retire. Just lookin' at his hands let me know he's been workin' hard all his life," Josh said.

"That's true, sir. But it's Aunt Martha that rules the roost and if she says retire, they'll retire."

Both men smiled at the deputies last statement and Josh walked over to where General was stalled. The men talked as General was saddled and the halter and lead rope placed on Windy's head. It was time for them to once again head west.

It was as Josh finished with Windy that the deputy extended his hand to Josh. "I wanna thank ya again for what ya did for my kin," the deep voiced deputy said as they firmly shook each others hand. "Pardon me for not tellin' ya earlier, my names George Robinson. Ben's my fathers brother."

Josh led General and Windy from the stable to the street and then climbed on General's back. As he rode off, he turned and waved to deputy George still standing in the livery entrance. Riding through town Josh passed a man that tipped his hat as he passed. Josh returned the gesture. A woman said "good morning" to him and he had returned "mornin' ma'am". That's what it had to be, he thought. It had been too early when he was on the street walking to Millie's. The town just wasn't awake yet. He smiled a wide smile and was glad the city wasn't as bad as he thought it was before.

As Mount Pleasant disappeared in the east, Josh thought of his stop in Texarkana. It was the only city he knew of that was actually a part of two states, half in Arkansas and half in Texas divided only by a main street common to both parts of the city. He shook his head and thought if it had been up to him, the entire city would have been in Arkansas. Texas was big enough.

Buzzards circled in the cloudless blue sky in the distance. An injured or dying animal was bound to be the reason for their gathering, he surmised. He hoped that was the reason for he'd encountered enough human disaster to last the rest of this journey homeward.

As General, Windy and Josh continued west, Josh's mind again began to wander. He thought of the pretty Melissa in her light yellow dress and wondered if he'd see her again when he got to Fort Worth. He thought of her long blond hair and how it moved in the breeze and how she seemed to float as she walked. He had never thought about a girl before the way he thought of Melissa, but he enjoyed watching her as she went about her business in his minds eye. He watched her but saw Bonnie's face.

An approaching rider brought him back to the present and Josh wondered what would happen now. To his surprise, the cowboy said nothing as they passed, just touched the brim of his hat as did Josh and both continued on their way. "Must be an early riser from Mount Pleasant," he said aloud and turned quickly in his saddle to see if the cowboy had heard him. He hadn't. "Yep, he's from Mount Pleasant."

As from Little Rock to Texarkana and Texarkana to Mount Pleasant, the trail the threesome traveled seemed endless. More and more often Josh would stand in the stirrups to give his backside a rest. That in itself let one know the ride he was on was long for as a sergeant in the cavalry during the war, Josh had ridden for days on end to get to where the battles were being fought or to escape the pursuit of a Union cavalry unit after a failed assault.

He stopped at a small creek for fresh water and to allow the horses to drink. He swapped the saddle and bridal from General to Windy and then sat in the shade of a small live oak tree. He watched the horses graze on the deep green grass that lined both sides of the creek. He also saw a red tailed hawk dive toward the ground and as it rose back into the clear blue sky saw it had a small rabbit clutched in its talons. He saw cattle grazing on both sides of the trail and wondered if these were the charge of the cowboy he'd passed earlier. He got up and walked around to stretch his legs and back before he got back in the saddle. As he walked, General followed. Windy, on the other hand, kept her nose in the grass.

As he rode on to the west he passed another stage relay station, but didn't stop. He just waved to the attendant and continued on his way. As the sun began to set on the far west side of this Texas prairie turning the ground to a golden brown, he saw in the distance the city called Sulphur Springs.

The heat of the day had given way to a cool evening and a soft summer breeze. As he entered town, he could see the residents milling around in the streets and speaking to each other as they passed. The benches in a small park were filled with gossiping women who watched their children as they played in the grass. A couple of young boys and a tomboy were climbing in one of the live oaks that shaded the park area and an irritated young mother was scolding her pigtailed daughter and telling her to come down from the tree.

Josh stopped where two men stood talking and asked where the livery stable was located. They pointed south and said, "At the far end of town next to the stage depot." Josh touched the brim of his hat and rode on. Windy's head moved from side to side as did Josh's taking in the sights of the busy city, each seeing that some stores were open and residents still shopped. Everywhere people were talking to each other, engrossed in their conversations and enjoying the cool of the early evening.

The owner of the livery walked out as Josh approached and took the lead rope Josh held and led General to a stall. He opened a stall gate for Windy and Josh led her in.

"Long day of riding?" the owner asked.

"Yep. It's been a long day, so give 'em some oats and all the hay they can eat, and a good brushin'. How much will it be for their keep?"

"Six bits apiece," the owner said.

As Josh pulled the saddle from Windy's back, he asked, "Lot of people out there on the street. What's goin' on?"

"Nothin' special. Happens every night this time of year. Guess everybody just likes everybody else," the owner said with a smile on his face. "Not many traveling through here come with two horses. You traveling a long distance?"

"Come a long way and got a long way to go. I'm headed home to Lincoln County, New Mexico Territory. Been fightin' in the war four years and I'm goin' home and stayin' put."

"I'm Rhett Whitlock," the livery owner said as Josh placed his saddle on the rack. "What name do ya go by?"

"Joshua Tidwell, but most call me Josh."

"You related to the Tidwell's of Fort Worth?"

"No, sir. The Liam Tidwell's of Lincoln. Got a bath house here in town."

"Yes, sir. Everything you'll need for the evening is at the Inn. Ya passed it comin' up here. Ya can get a bath, eat some supper, have a drink and get some sleep all in the same place. Good food too."

Josh thanked Rhett for his help and walked to the open doors. Leaving the livery, he noticed the stagecoach setting in front of the depot and thought of Jamie and Buck and wondered how far they were behind him.

The Inn was just as Rhett had said. Josh found everything he needed there. He took his bed roll containing his clean clothes and his saddle bags to his room. He removed his clothes, confederate grey uniform and duster from his bed roll and hung them in the clothes closet hoping some of the wrinkles might fall out. He closed the closet doors and walked out of his room and down to the dining room.

A thick, rare bone end steak, mashed potatoes, carrots, string beans, coffee and two beers occupied his time for over an hour. He liked the little old lady that was his server for she kept his coffee cup full and repeatedly asked if she could get him another beer. She was very pleasant and performed her job well, but Josh could tell it was either time for a break or close to time to go home. She seemed tired. When he finished dinner, he paid the cashier for his meal and then looked for his waitress. Her big smile was all the thanks he needed for the dollar tip he handed her as he walked from the dining room and into the bar.

There weren't as many people in the bar as Josh had expected. With all the people on the street, Josh couldn't believe that more of the men weren't visiting the bar. It was really a nice place with brightly colored curtains on the windows, leather padded chairs around the tables, a spotless mirror behind the bar and a highly polished mahogany bar top. Behind the bar on shelves in front of the mirror were bottles containing anything you might think of to drink. He had never before seen such a well stocked bar.

There were eight men in the bar. Four sat at one table and two each at two other tables. A young woman was standing by one of the tables and Josh knew she worked here for she wore a bright red dress that would only be seen in a bar. Seeing Josh enter, she walked toward him with a big smile on her face.

The bartender was a tall man with a full head of thick black hair. His face was long and narrow as was his body. A thick black mustache covered his upper lip and half of his mouth.

"What can I get for ya, friend? We got just about anything ya can think of ta drink," he said as he stood facing Josh. He was bigger than Josh had thought for he towered over him.

"Bourbon, and ya can leave the bottle."

The woman dressed in red stopped at the bar beside him and said, "Gonna buy me a drink, stranger? My name's Lacy. What's yours?"

"What'll ya have? The name's Josh."

"What you're having will be fine."

"Bartender. Bring two glasses, will you please." Josh was happy she was drinking bourbon for during the war he had been in a bar in

Georgia. When he had asked the woman who approached him there what she wanted, she ordered champagne. It only came by the bottle and he was broke when he finished paying for it.

Lacy and Josh talked the usual bar talk for a bit and then she asked "Anything else I can do for ya, Josh?" Her eyes were big and bluish green and not a strand of her dark brown hair was out of place. He knew at once what she was asking him, but paused before he answered. It had been a long time since he had been with a woman and he almost agreed to go with her, but something told him to leave her alone.

"Thanks for the offer, but I don't think so, not tonight."

"Your loss, cowboy. You don't know what you're missing." She picked up her glass and downed the bourbon in one swallow, smiled, and turned back to the men at the tables.

She sure didn't seem to float when she walked and her hair didn't move at all, Josh thought. He picked up his bottle and walked back to his room.

As Josh sat up in bed, he swung around and put his feet on the floor and saw that the sun was up and he heard the town coming to life on the street below. He had over slept again, but this time he knew why. Too much food and too much bourbon. The bottle he had purchased in the bar was on the table beside the bed and it was over half full. He hadn't had as much to drink as he thought and picked up the bottle and placed it in his saddle bags. He dressed in his clean blue shirt and dark pants, rolled his dirty clothes, his uniform and duster back in his bed roll and placed it next to his saddle bags. He walked to the wash basin, poured water into it and washed himself. The bath he had taken after leaving the bar had felt good and he was ready for another day of westward travel. He thought about the fact that most people were under the impression that cowboys and travelers didn't take baths. Some didn't, but he wasn't one of them. The war had taught him to take advantage of his surroundings and he felt that meant baths too.

He stopped in the restaurant on his way out of the hotel and had two cups of coffee, but had resisted the awesome smell of breakfast. He had eaten enough the night before.

On his way to the livery stable he greeted those he passed on the street with a tip of his hat and upon arriving said, "Good morning, Rhett."

Rhett was busy brushing Windy and as he continued with his chore turned and returned Josh's greeting.

"How far is it from here ta Fort Worth, Rhett?"

"Oh, let's see. It's eighty miles here ta Dallas and 'bout twenty or so from Dallas ta Fort Worth. Guess you got 'bout a hundred miles ta go. What are you looking for in Fort Worth?"

"A pretty girl, Rhett. A real pretty girl." Josh finished saddling General and made sure Windy was ready to go and then led the two horses out of the stable. The two men talked for a minute or two, then shook hands and Josh climbed on General. A little spur to General's flank and a "Come on Windy" and the three again headed homeward.

Chapter Four
Fort Worth Bound

Josh did some quick figuring and thought he could make Fort Worth in two days if he pushed his horses hard or three days if he took his time and took it easy on General and Windy. They were his best friends on this journey, so he decided on three days. He smiled as he thought that Melissa could wait an extra day to see his smiling face again.

The farther west they rode the more sparse the vegetation became. Prairie grass was the predominant growth and cattle roaming freely were growing fat eating on what looked to Josh to be dry or dying grass. The number of cattle increased the closer they got to Dallas, and chap clad cowboys could be seen mingling with and keeping watch over the herds.

Josh stopped at a watering hole to change horses and allow the two to drink. One of the cowhands saw Josh and rode in his direction.

"Need a hand there, partner?" he asked as he rode up to Josh. He rode a young buckskin and seemed much at home sitting in his saddle.

"Just watering the horses and changing mounts," Josh answered.

The rider wore a plaid shirt, stovepipe chaps, a tan narrow brimmed felt hat and what looked like an old, well used Navy Colt on his right side. It was waist high, so Josh thought he would have trouble getting the gun from its holster in a hurry. How strange it was that someone who spent most of his life out doors underneath the sun would wear a narrow brimmed hat that failed to shade his entire face, he thought as the two continued to talk. "How far is it ta Dallas from here?" Josh asked.

"'Bout sixteen miles. That where yer headed? It's an easy ride. You'll be there before ya know it."

"Thanks, friend," Josh said as me mounted Windy. I'm headed for Fort Worth so I got 'bout thirty-five miles to go." He touched the brim of his hat, nodded and was on his way. He spurred the mare and brought her up to an easy lope and kept her at that gait for about half a mile then slowed her to a trot. General followed willingly and seemed to enjoy the easy run. They slowed to a walk with the approach of a buckboard carrying two adults and three kids. A family on their way home, he surmised. The men exchanged nods to each other as they passed, but no words were spoken. The drivers wife had an uneasy look about her and Josh didn't want to add to her distress. The driver's young toe headed daughter, riding in the back of the buckboard stuck out her tongue at Josh as he went by. The two boys sat quietly as they watched the actions of their younger sister. The older of the two stuck his hand in front of his sisters face and she pushed his hand away. It was evident to Josh that this young lady got away with a lot more than the boys did.

The look on the woman's face as he passed brought back the words Buckskin Jones had told him while they repaired the stagecoach wheel east of Little Rock. He had said the roads were dangerous because of outlaws and renegade soldiers since the end of the war. It was apparent this woman firmly believed this to be true. How different it seemed now going home than what it had as he headed east to the war. People all stopped to talk as they passed before, but now they just kept to themselves. If the roads were so full of outlaws, where were they? He had passed few people on his journey and none were outlaws. Indians didn't count he thought as he continued toward home.

The heat of the day was again upon the threesome as they traveled westward. Not a hint of a breeze could be felt and the dust kicked up by the buckboard just floated in the air. Josh pulled the old piece of shirt he used for a handkerchief from his pocket, folded it into a triangle and then tied it around his neck. He rotated the knot he had tied to the back of his neck and pulled the cloth over his mouth and nose. It remained there until the dust had settled and the air was again breathable. It was evident it hadn't rained in this area for quite a few days.

The ride had been long, but a town could be seen in the distance and Josh thought it must be Dallas. He knew he could make the town by dark and would spend the night there and get an early start for Fort Worth in the morning.

As he rode on toward the town, the sun dropped behind behind clouds on the distant horizon and created a beautiful sunset. The golds, yellows, reds and purples made possible by the sun shining through the moisture in the clouds were almost as pretty as the many sunsets he had witnessed from his home in Lincoln. It wouldn't be long before he would again see the sun set on his home and he vowed he would watch the sun set from the porch of his own home until he died of old age. He had traveled far, had seen things he felt no man should ever have to see and upon reaching the land where he had been raised, would put down roots and raise his own family.

Dallas seemed to Josh to have changed quite a bit since he had passed through over four years earlier on his way to fight in the war. It was much bigger and there were many more residents rather than just the wide spot in the road he remembered. Now there were stores, restaurants, and even a small hotel where he hoped he'd be able to spend the night. With General and Windy settled in the livery for the night, Josh walked to the hotel with bed roll and saddle bags in hand.

He hadn't noticed the name of the hotel, just knew he wanted to eat and find a clean, soft bed in which to get some sleep. The long days ride had taken its toll and he was tired, dirty and ready to sit on something sitting solidly on a floor rather than in the constant motion of a saddle. As he walked into the hotel, he saw a woman standing on the far side of the room.

"Good evening, young man. Looking for a room, are you?"

Josh nodded his head in answer to the woman's question. The woman was a little more than middle aged as her hair piled neatly on her head was turning grey on the sides. She wore a blue dress with long sleeves and a collar that tightly hugged her neck. White lace adorned the collar and sleeves and a matching belt was around her waist.

"Step over to the counter and we'll fix you right up."

He walked to the counter, dropped his bed roll and saddle bags on the floor and signed the register. He looked from the register to the woman and asked, "The dining room still open?"

"Yes. And you can get a bath at the end of that hallway, if you so choose."

"Thank you, ma'am," Josh said as the woman handed him a room key.

He must be dirtier than he thought for the woman to have made such a statement. He didn't know whether to be embarrassed or angry, but she had only relayed to him what she saw, so he let it go.

"Second door on the left," she said. "It faces the street, but it should be quiet. All the excitement happened last night."

"What happened last night?"

"Couple of cowboys from Fort Worth came over and tried to rob the bank. There was a lot of shooting and one of the boy's got killed. The other was wounded, but he'll heal up and be able to stand trial. They'll hang him for sure to set an example for the others that might think of robbing our bank. That bullet hole there above the door came from a stray shot," she said while pointing to the hole.

"How much longer will the dining room be open?"

"Long enough for you to have a bath. A couple of more hours at least."

Once this woman set her mind on something, it was really set. She seemed to be the proverbial matriarch and Josh knew she could bite a horse shoe nail in half.

As he sat soaking in the bathtub, he thought of the pretty Melissa and how he hoped he would see her again the following day. He remembered her pretty face, small waist and hands, and her air of confidence.

He imagined the softness of her skin and hair and remembered the fragrance of the perfume she wore. As he continued washing, he could think of no flaws. The young lady seemed perfect.

Josh finished his bath, dressed in the clean clothes he had washed in a stream where they had stopped for water and walked to the dining room. As he passed through the hotel entry, he saw the woman hotel clerk watching him pass.

"Big improvement," she said as he passed.

The dining room was nearly empty for the hour was late, but Josh didn't care. He was hungry and he was accustomed to eating by himself for most of his meals had been eaten on the trail. His dinner of roast beef, potatoes, and lima beans had gone down good, but the cobbler he had for dessert was so good that he had a second helping. The peach cobbler had tasted almost as good as that his grandmother made at home.

Having finally finished his meal he got up from the table and walked to the cashier. Instantly his waitress started clearing the table. She had been standing patiently in the doorway to the kitchen waiting for the opportunity to complete her work. It was evident she was ready to go home. He was so tired he couldn't have told anyone what she looked like. He walked to his room and fell into bed.

When leaving the hotel the following morning, Josh saw the woman he had talked to the night before.

"Mornin' ma'am. Have a nice day."

"Where are you traveling to today, young man?" she asked while accidentally showing a smile.

"Fort Worth, ma'am. Only goin' as far as Fort Worth today. I'm going to see a friend that lives there."

"Who's the friend? Maybe I know them and can tell you where they might be found."

"Melissa Ryon. I met her in Little Rock and she said to stop by on my way home."

"She'll not be there. Fort Worth has fallen on hard times since the war and most of the businesses are closed. Most of the people there are cowboys pushing cattle up the Chisholm Trail or outlaws. The permanent residents have left and moved here or to Abilene. The town now seems to be full of outlaws, cattle drovers and those that can't afford to leave. But I am sure the Ryon's left. Most all the business owners have," she said again.

"Thanks for the information," Josh said not really wanting to hear what she had said. He tipped his hat walked out and up the street to the livery.

He was on the trail early and noticed right off that General's gait was smooth and didn't seem to bother his backside as much as Windy's gait had the day before. They were both good horses, but General had been Josh's friend since birth and the bond between them could not be put into words. The big black stud had countless times carried him from danger during the war and his reward would come when they reached home. He would be turned loose and allowed to roam the ranch as he pleased. Hopefully he would find a mare he really liked and give Josh another colt to raise.

As the three continued traveling west, a feeling of sadness came over Josh. It wasn't the fact that Fort Worth had fallen on hard times that bothered him. It was not knowing where to find Melissa that was the cause of his down and out spirit. Hopefully he would find someone in the city that knew where she had gone.

The ride on to Fort Worth seemed to take forever even though Josh was no longer in a hurry or friendly state of mind. The fact that he really didn't know the young woman made no difference. It was as if, in his mind, they had know each other since childhood and he couldn't believe she would leave town and not leave him word as to where she was going.

He shook his head trying to clear his mind and wondered what was bothering him so much. In reality he knew she felt nothing for him for she didn't know him. The smile he had received from her had only been a courtesy and it was in his own mind that he had made something else of it.

He tried to remove her from his mind by thinking of home, but couldn't. Whether he liked it or not she would be a part of his thinking until, once again, they saw each other.

Fort Worth was as the hotel manager in Dallas had said. It was nearly deserted and would have been had it not been for the soldiers from the fort and the cattle drovers that were in town while the herds of cattle they drove north to market rested in the stockyards below the fort to the north. The fort overlooked the Trinity River and had originally been built as one of ten forts that marked the western Texas frontier. It had seen a massive influx of new residents, but with the Civil War had witnessed a dramatic loss of inhabitants and been taken over by cowboys and outlaws. The only law was that the soldiers from the fort could provide.

The street leading to the fort seemed now to be the main artery of what was left of the city. Fort Worth was now actually a fort named Worth. Some of the closed stores had been destroyed by fire and others that still stood were used for saloons, eateries, and make shift sleeping accommodations.

A drunk cowboy feeling his oats nearly fell out of a saloon doorway and, seeing Josh, pulled his pistol and fired in his direction. Josh dropped the lead rope to Windy, wheeled General hard to the right and charged the drunk cowboy. As General ran into the drunk, Josh slid from the saddle and landed beside him where he laid on the ground. As the cowboy tried to return to his feet, Josh pulled his Navy Colt and smacked the drunk up along side the head putting him back on the ground.

"Anyone know this drunk?" Josh asked those who were watching what had transpired. No one answered his question.

Two cowboys were approaching and trying to see what was going on. Seeing their friend lying on the ground with blood running from his head got their blood up and they demanded to know who it was that hurt him.

Josh looked the bigger of the two straight in the eye and said, "I did, friend. You got somethin' ta say 'bout it?"

The big cowboy reached out to grab Josh and in an instant found himself staring down the barrel of a Navy Colt. Startled by the rapid appearance of the handgun set him back on his heels and both he and his friend half raised their hands and let it be known they wanted no part of what Josh would do if they pushed the situation.

An army sergeant ran up and quickly took control of the situation. His blue uniform was dusty and well worn, but his deep voice demanded attention and his presence calmed the action of the cowboys.

"All right cowboy, calm down. And you, sir, put that gun away. We'll have no more trouble here or I'll place you all under arrest and throw you in the stockade."

The cowboy on the ground began to stir and stumbled to his feet. "Who hit me?" he demanded.

The sergeant pointed to Josh.

"Oh, yeah. I remember. I tried to shoot your hat off, stranger," he said while rubbing his head. "I think I was run over by a horse too."

"You damn near blew my head off, you idiot. Why would you try something like that in your condition?" Josh questioned.

"Just for the fun of it. I was bored."

Josh said nothing, just closed his fist, hit the cowboy in the jaw and watched him topple to the ground again. His friends said and did nothing.

The sergeant told the cowboy's to pick up their friend and get him off the street. "If I see any of you again tonight, it's the stockade. Understand?" He turned to Josh and continued, "You, son, you come with me now."

The sergeant waited as Josh collected General and Windy and then the sergeant joined him and they walked toward the fort.

"What is it you want from me?" Josh asked as they walked.

"It's not for me to say. Yer gonna talk to my commanding officer and he'll let you know what it is that he needs. I'm just a sergeant and know when to keep my mouth shut, but I think you'll be interested in what he has to say. You just look the type."

"What type is that? What the heck are you talking about, sergeant?"

"Patience my boy. You'll find out in just a minute."

Inside the fort was like walking into another room. One room messy, as was the city, and the other well kept and orderly.

As Josh and the sergeant approached the orderly room where the sergeants commanding officer was quartered, Josh asked, "Have you ever heard of a man by the name of Jason Tidwell or a young woman named Melissa Ryon?"

"Tidwell? Sure. Everyones heard of him. He's owns the biggest ranch in these parts and raises the most cattle too. As for the woman, can't say that I know her. Why do you ask?"

"My names Tidwell and just wanted to know if somehow we're related. The woman I met in Little Rock."

"You from these parts?"

"No, farther to the west. I'm from Lincoln County, New Mexico Territory. I'm on my way home from the war. On hearin' my name, a couple of men have asked if I was related, so I thought I'd try to find out."

"Fought for the Confederacy, did ya?" the sergeant asked. He noticed Josh tense as he spoke and continued, "Take it easy, son. The war's over now and I don't care what side ya fought for."

"How'd you know? Lot's from these parts fought for the north."

"That's true," the sergeant said. "But not many of the northern soldiers wore holsters with the letters CSA stamped into the leather." He smiled a wide smile and prided himself on being so observant and for making a good impression on the man with whom he walked.

The sergeant stopped and yelled at a private and told him to take the horses from Josh and bed them down in the stables. "Bring his bed roll and saddle bags to the orderly room and make sure nothing ends up missing from them. Understand? It's your hide if you don't mind my words," the sergeant barked.

"I still don't know why I'm here, sergeant. What the heck have you got up your sleeve?"

"Patience, my boy. You'll find out momentarily."

The two men climbed the five stairs to the porch level of the wooden building, walked across it to the door and walked in. As they entered, the sergeant snapped to attention and remained at attention in front of a desk occupied by a captain that didn't seem to happy to have been interrupted.

"Sergeant Tadlock to see the commanding officer, if you please," he said while remaining at attention.

As the captain rose from his chair he said, "At ease, sergeant."

Josh could see right off that the captain was a career soldier for his uniform was surely custom made. The brass buttons on the jacket of his uniform shined and his boots were highly polished. The sergeant, on the other hand was nearing the end of his military career. His uniform had come straight from the quartermaster and his boots, though shined, showed the dust and dirt of a working soldier.

The captain knocked on the commandants door, disappeared momentarily, then reappeared and motioned for the sergeant to enter the office.

Sergeant Tadlock motioned for Josh to follow and as he entered the room marched to the desk on the far side of the office and snapped to attention. "Sergeant Tadlock reporting, sir."

"At ease, Bill," the grey headed colonel said from behind his desk. "Knock off all the military courtesy crap and tell me what you want. We've been friends far to long for you to start respecting my rank now. What is it you want and who's your friend there?"

The colonel, too, seemed to Josh to be close to retirement age. And, unlike the captain, wore a uniform that betrayed the fact that he was a working officer and got out in the field among his men.

"You recall the talk we had the other night, sir, the one about needin' someone to ride herd on this place? Well, sir, I think I've found him." With those words he pointed to Josh. "He busted a drunks head for takin' a shot at him rather than shootin' back and killin' the kid. And he faced down two of the drunks friends without firin' a shot or startin' a fight. Seems to me he's just what we been lookin' for, wouldn't you say, sir?"

The colonel was a tall man, much taller than the sergeant Josh could see as the man rose from the chair, rounded his desk and walked toward him. He extended his hand as he approached and Josh shook his hand firmly.

"Young man, I'm John Bradley and we have a problem here. The military can only be employed to help the citizens if they are accosted by Indians, an invading army from the south, or, in some cases, when a town is attacked by a large band of outlaws. But, sad to say, we really have no right under the law to ride herd on the lawlessness that now plagues the streets of Fort Worth. It's a matter of civil law rather than military law. You understand don't you, son?"

Josh nodded his head in affirmation, but questioned "what has this got to do with me, sir?"

"Just this, son. We've sent for a new lawman to clean up this town, but he's been delayed and we're unsure when he might arrive to assume his duties. Until he arrives, we need someone to assume the responsibilities of town marshall."

Josh thought of Jamie Coulter back in Little Rock and how he had said that a lawman's late arrival was putting him behind schedule and he wondered if this lawman could be the same person the colonel waited for here. He eyed the colonel and then the sergeant and shook his head.

"You know nothin' 'bout me, sir. How can ya offer such a position to someone ya just met? You've no idea how I'll react under the pressure of a marshall's badge," Josh said in a questioning voice.

"I know you rode in a cavalry unit during the war and I'd be willing to bet you commanded and led men into battle. I can tell you are a fair man because you listen before you speak and from what Tadlock has told me, you have a cool head on your shoulders and think before you act. Now really, son, what else do I really need to know. As sure as I'm standin' here, I know you'll do a good job. What do you say, son?"

"Yeah, Josh. What do ya say?" the sergeant added.

"I don't know? Let me sleep on it and I'll let ya know in the mornin'."

"Fair enough," Colonel Bradley said and Sergeant Tadlock grunted his approval.

As Josh and Tadlock left the office, he found his bed roll and saddle bags in the outer office. The captain pointed to them as the two came into his view upon exiting the colonel's office. They had not been touched and Josh felt the sergeants words and actions were something to which everyone in the fort paid attention.

They billeted Josh with the non commissioned officers and in the morning he accepted the job he'd been offered with the understanding that the arrival of a real lawman would terminate his employment immediately. He had to get home sooner rather than later.

Chapter Five

Sheriff Tidwell

The star that Colonel Bradley had pinned to his shirt was just a cheap piece of metal that in itself was light, but the responsibilities it brought with it were more than heavy. It could easily get him killed or could get someone else killed and would feel no different no matter the way it turned out. As Josh left the stable on General, Windy acted nervous and didn't want to be left behind. "Your turn tomorrow," he said as he looked back to the pinto, then turned and rode out of the fort. He made sure the star on his chest could be easily seen and had decided earlier that if something was going to happen as a result of the badge, better sooner than later.

Josh kept General at a slow even pace as he rode down the main street and he advertised the fact that there was a new law in town. He hoped that he would be challenged early not so much to show his expertise with a gun as to let everyone know that the drunken escapades of the cowboys would no longer be tolerated.

His hopes were granted for as he rode, the barrel of a rifle appeared in an upstairs window of a makeshift hotel and the shot that followed the sighting passed near General's right ear. Josh jumped from the saddle, ran through the doors of the hotel and up the stairs to the second floor. He broke the door to the room from its hinges and charged into the room. The startled cowboy sat on the edge of the bed still holding the rifle in his hands. He didn't try to use it and Josh pulled his Navy Colt and hit the cowboy, clad only in his red long johns, hard in the mouth and then pushed him through the open window. He followed him through the window to the balcony then hit the cowboy again and threw him from the balcony to the ground below. He looked over the edge of the balcony and then climbed back through the window. To the woman that held the covers tightly around her neck he said, "You want to see him again, you'll find him in the fort stockade. Bring money. It'll cost to get him out."

The woman said nothing, still in shock from what she had just seen. This new marshall meant business and there was no doubt in her mind that things around Fort Worth were going to change. For the better or for the worse she didn't know, but things around this town would surely change.

Josh walked down the stairs to the first floor and told the clerk to add the broken door to the cowboys bill. The cowboy's face was bloody from the nose down and Josh helped him to his feet. Though still dazed from the two blows to the head, Josh told him to head for the fort, whistled for General and rode behind the barefoot, long john clad cowboy. People laughed as he passed and Josh thought the embarrassment brought about by his actions would keep him from a repeat performance.

For the following two weeks similar tactics were employed by other drunk cowboys on the new marshall and he used his same tactic of cracking heads. The more heads he cracked the more the account held by Colonel Bradley into which their fines were deposited grew. It paid Josh a descent wage with enough left over to cover the wages of a real lawman for a couple of weeks when and if he arrived. If no money was available to pay their fines, they worked cleaning up the city and it wasn't long before the town again looked nice enough to live in.

Josh was ready to head for home. He felt his time here had been well spent, but wanted to go home and even more than that find where Melissa had gone. One of the empty buildings in town had the Ryon name on it. The sign above the door read, Ryon's Emporium - Tom Ryon, proprietor. Who was Tom Ryon? Was he a father, brother, or cousin. Or could he be a husband? The thought of the latter caused Josh some mental discomfort for this was the last thing he wanted to find. He had built her up in his mind to the point that she could belong to no other. She was his.

A stage coach entered town from the west and Josh immediately recognized Jamie Coulter sitting in the drivers seat, but Buck Jones could not be seen. Jamie acknowledged Josh as he passed, but kept the horses at a lope as they approached the fort. Jamie raced through the fort gates and skidded the stage to a stop in front of the dispensary. "Hurry men. Buck's been shot and we gotta get him inside quick. It was Indians that did it and he's got the arrow in his chest to prove it."

Josh rode up as they carried Buck into the building. He could see the arrow protruding from the mans chest. He followed them into the dispensary and then asked Jamie what had happened.

"Well, I'll be horn swoggled," Jamie said seeing the star on Josh's chest. "How the heck did they get that star on yer chest, boy? Thought you was in a hurry ta git home."

"Guess I wasn't in as big a hurry as I thought."

"How long ya been marshall?"

"'Bout two weeks. I told 'em I'd work 'til a real lawman showed up."

"Hey, remember that little gal you was so sweet on. She's married, son. Hauled her and the husband to Albuquerque 'bout three weeks ago. Three weeks? Yeah, it was three weeks ago."

The doctor, an army major, cut the arrow from Buck's chest and said he would be up and around in no time for the arrow had hit nothing vital.

"He must be unconscious due to the knot on his head. The arrow has nothing to do with it. How did he get the knot?" the doctor asked.

Jamie just shook his head for he didn't know where the bump had come from.

"He fell from the seat of the stage to the ground when he was shot, but he never got a bump before. He's fell off lots of times, but nothin' like this happened," Jamie said. They would have to wait for Buck to wake up to find out what had happened to his head.

Josh had a good feeling when he heard Buck would be okay and he knew that Jamie would be a bunch easier to get along with too. It was hearing Melissa was a married woman that got him so upset. He turned away and walked slowly to where he had tied General. He rubbed on the horse's neck, then took the reins in hand and mounted the big stud. He hoped he would find some poor cowboy doing something wrong to help take his mind off the woman.

The next few days were somewhat less than exciting for the new sheriff of Fort Worth. As time passed, he thought less and less of Melissa. The little Mexican girl that he met two nights prior also helped to wash the memories from his mind.

Six weeks later when Ben Wright, a real marshall, rode into town on the weekly stage, the town was quiet and peaceful and Josh was addressed as Marshall Tidwell or Mr. Tidwell. Ben Wright was a town tamer by reputation and wondered why he had been summoned to such a peaceful town as Fort Worth. He accepted the the job of town marshall, but within three months left to tame a new town somewhere in the Arizona Territory. Two months prior to Marshall Wright's departure, Josh Tidwell, now too a town tamer, left Fort Worth and disappeared into the west riding a big black stud with a pinto mare in tow.

Word of the job he had done in taming a Texas town quickly spread and, thanks to Colonel Bradley and Sergeant Tadlock, requests for his services came from many different states and many different cities. All were sent to Fort Worth and taken to Colonel Bradley or Sergeant Tadlock. In turn, they would take the requests and forward them to Fort Stanton, a small army post about ten miles to the southwest of Lincoln, New Mexico, with a note requesting they be hand carried to the Tidwell Ranch. The requests were carried by a dispatch rider that made a routine run from fort to fort on a regular basis.

Four months had passed before Josh made it back to Lincoln County, New Mexico Territory. He had left his home a young man of twenty-one and returned to his home at twenty-six, a veteran of a war and now a town tamer. It would be hard for his parents to conceive of the reasons that caused the changes that war and his work had brought upon their son. He left home a young man to fight in the Civil War was all they would remember. But buried deep inside were the scars left from watching so many friends and comrades die and the woman he loved, lost.

Chapter Six
Albuquerque

The old homestead looked better than when he had left. The house and barn looked to have been freshly painted and Josh couldn't see a fence in need of repair. As he rode closer to the house, a woman walked out and into the front yard. She shaded her eyes from the noon sun and watched to see who it was that rode toward the house. Her reddish brown hair had been braided and twisted into a bun that sat on top of her head. Her green dress and white apron moved gently in the easy breeze that kept the day pleasant. As the rider got closer, her eyes suddenly widened and she called out, "Liam, get out here and in a hurry. Our son is home," she exclaimed.

"What's that you say, Rebecca? Who comin' to the house?" As he walked from the house and got a good look at the approaching rider he stopped, looked toward the sky and said, "Thank you, God, for bringing my boy home safe." Both Rebecca and Liam hurried to their son's side as he stepped down from General.

"It's good to have you home, son," she said as she gave him a big hug. "We've got so much to tell you and so many questions to ask that we will be talking constantly for the next week." She smiled a big smile and kissed his cheek as his father shook his hand firmly.

"I've been lookin' for ya for a couple of weeks now, son. I'm glad ya made it home safe."

Josh turned to General and loosened the saddle cinch and pulled the saddle and blanket from his back and placed it on the hitching rail. He tied the lead rope to Windy to the rail, removed the bridal from General's head and, as promised, set him free. As he did, he asked his father, "Two weeks ago, huh. What made you think I'd be home then?"

"We heard what you did in Fort Worth, son, and when we heard you'd disappeared, we felt you'd be headin' this way."

"You always did know what I was about to do, dad. Guess you've still got the knack."

"Let's go into the kitchen and I'll get us some coffee and we can talk there," his mother said interrupting their conversation. "You hungry, boy?" As she walked to the kitchen, she stopped to pick up some papers from a counter. "These papers came for ya over the last couple of weeks," she said handing them to her son.

They were requests for his services and he threw them in the stove.

"If you got some made, I could sure eat some you your peach cobbler."

"You and Ted are so much alike, she said as she poured the three cups of coffee. He loves cobbler just like you, son."

"Ted?" Josh questioned. "Who's Ted?"

"He's a boy that just showed up here one day lookin' for work and just stayed. Me and your mom kinda adopted the boy and treat him like one of the family. He's like you, son. He's a hard worker and don't quit 'til the jobs done. You'll like him when you meet him. He should be back in a couple of days. He's out checkin' the stock in the high country."

"Let's not talk about Ted," Josh's mother said as she sat a plate of cobbler in front of him and handed him a fork. As she sat down at the kitchen table, she continued, "I want to know about you and hear what you've been up too."

"What I've been up to," Josh said while shaking his head. "They're million dollar memories I wouldn't give a plug nickel to relive, mom. All my travelin' has got me is nights full of bad dreams of war and a reputation that some stupid cowboy wanting to make a reputation for himself will want to challenge. Not much of a future for the cowboy or for me.

As the days passed, Ted came home and Josh and he became good friends and worked around the ranch together. Ted was much like Josh in manner and stature. He was tall, dark complected due to long hours in the sun with dark blond hair and a friendly face. Josh always said to him that he was glad he was a part of the family and how he appreciated him watching out for his folks while he had been gone. From sun up until sun down the two worked side by side and everything was fine until his mother asked at dinner one evening if he remembered Bonnie Davis. Bonnie was a girl from a neighboring ranch that had always been sweet on Josh when he was younger.

"Yeah, I remember her. She's the one with the blond hair and pigtails that used to follow me around like a lost puppy."

"Really," Ted exclaimed. "Been a long time since ya seen her, huh? She don't wear pigtails no more and she surely don't look like no lost puppy. No, sir. She is really a looker now."

"Ted," Josh's mother said. "You mind your manners, boy. Bonnie is a real nice girl. She comes by every so often to visit and see if we have received any word from you, Josh. You know you could have written a little more often."

It was a couple of days later that Josh saw the surrey drive up to the house from a field about a quarter mile from the house. He watched the young blond dressed in a pretty white dress step from the surrey and walk to the house. It had to be Bonnie, Josh thought, and a good reason for him to stay away from the house. Ted, unlike Josh, wanted to see Bonnie and seeing her approach the house had headed that way himself.

It was near sunset when Josh saw Ted escort Bonnie to the surrey and mount his buckskin to accompany her on her way home. When they disappeared into the trees, he whistled for General and rode to the house.

"Your dinner is on the stove," his mother said as he entered the house. "It was rude of you not to come in when you saw Bonnie was here."

Rebecca could tell that her son was growing more and more restless as he worked around the ranch. She had thought seeing Bonnie would calm his restlessness and just maybe light a fire in Josh that she was sure burned in Bonnie. If something didn't change soon, her son would be off and wandering again.

Word came from Albuquerque that the city was looking for a new marshall and Josh made up his mind he wanted the job. He longed for the action of a wide open city, the saloons, the fights, and the fact remained that Melissa was there. Until he found her and got answers to his questions, he would never rest.

Snow had fallen the night before Josh left. It was cold and the wind seemed to cut right through his clothes as he walked to the barn. His good-byes had been said and he asked his parents to remain in the house where it was warm. They were in their fifties and he didn't want them to catch cold or see the tears that now ran down his still tanned face. Ted had promised to stay and keep an eye on his parents and that gave him some solace as he saddled the big black stud and haltered Windy. He thought of leaving the pinto at the ranch, but she and the General were such friends that he decided she should come along. He placed his saddle bags behind the saddle, tied his bed roll on, stuck his foot in the stirrup and climbed aboard General. With Windy in tow, Josh waved to his parents standing in the window of their warm house and started off toward Lincoln.

As he entered the small pueblo he saw that it was bigger than when he left to fight in the war. Most of the buildings were constructed of adobe, but the newer buildings were built of wood. As he passed a store he heard his name being called.

"Josh. Josh Tidwell," someone called.

As he looked in the direction of the store he saw Bonnie. She wore long trousers and a fur lined buckskin heavy coat to keep out the cold. Her blond hair was half hidden by the brown felt hat she wore and her boots were covered with snow as she approached the General and Josh.

"You've been dodging me, Josh. Haven't seen you since you've been home and now you're leaving again. Was I that much of a pest when we were young?" Her face glowed with youth and happiness.

"Just thought it would be easier on both of us if I just stayed home," Josh answered. "And, yes, I am leaving again. Headed for Albuquerque."

"We heard they were looking for a sheriff, and I wondered if you would be the one to get it." She smiled widely and touched his hand and said, "I'll be here when you get back and next time I won't let you dodge me." Still smiling, she turned and walked back to the store. As she entered, she looked to see if he was watching her.

He was.

The farther down the mountain he rode, the warmer it got and soon he was having to shed some of his heavy clothing. First he removed his heavy coat and then the fur lined leather vest. It felt good for him to be able to stretch and move again rather than be confined under all that heavy clothing. He stopped and climbed down from General's back. He would walk for a bit and work the kinks out of his legs and back. His hand dropped to his gun and he pulled it and fired. He turned quickly to see if Windy was going to raise a fuss, but she paid little attention and just followed along behind General. He replaced the gun in its holster, raised his hand to waist level and then drew again, but didn't fire. Over and over he pulled the Navy Colt from its holster and each time it was done with a little more speed. Practice, his mother told him as a boy, made perfect. He was striving for more than perfection. He was striving to be the best.

Josh followed the Rio Grande north stopping only to eat and sleep. He wandered a bit, but always kept the river in sight because it was unseasonably hot in the desert below the mountains and he and the horses needed water. He was in a hurry again and it felt good to be rushing toward a new job in a new area with new people to meet and the answers to specific questions only one person could answer at the end of his journey.

He passed few travelers and those he did he couldn't understand anyway, so he kept pushing himself to the north. He had encountered a few villages along the river, small and all made up of Mexican inhabitants. Few spoke any gringo and Josh spoke no Mexican, so conversations had taken the form of hand gestures and finger pointing. Somehow, both the Mexicans and Josh had gotten their point across and all wore smiles as he departed following the river north. And best of all, he thought, neither he nor the horses went hungry for there was plenty of grass and Josh really liked the taste of tortillas and pinto beans.

Albuquerque was in the distance and Josh felt that he would be in the town within a half days ride. He stopped to have a bath prior to entering the pueblo. He sat on a rock to pull off his boots and socks, then removed his shirt and pants. He unbuttoned his long johns to the waist and then stepped into the water. It was then that he heard the giggling of two young Mexican girls hiding in the brush that watched him as he prepared to bathe. Feeling a little frisky, he walked to where the water was but knee deep and acted as if he would continue to undress. At that point, one of the young girls turned to leave, then paused and called to her friend to follow. She was being ignored so she reached down and grabbed her friends hair and pulled her from the view of Josh's bath. He took his hat off long enough to wash his hair. Then he shaved, dressed in his clean clothes his mother had laundered and pressed for him and then rode on to the town.

The town hall was one of the larger of the adobe buildings that made up the town of Albuquerque. He stooped over to get through the door and once inside saw two city employees seated at desks and could tell they wouldn't be able to answer his questions regarding employment as sheriff. He walked toward the nearest desk and told the man seated there that he was interested in the sheriff's job he heard was open. The older of the workers asked his name and when he said Josh Tidwell, not a sound could be heard.

"You're Josh Tidwell, the Fort Worth Tidwell? They say it was so quiet there when Ben Wright took over that he only lasted three months before he took off to some wild town in Arizona. Guess you cleaned up that town pretty good," the woman office worker said.

"When will someone be here I can talk to about the job opening," Josh asked.

"Later this afternoon. Probably around three o'clock would be a good time to catch 'em. It's been sort of bad around here lately and not everyone wants the job, so I don't guess you're going to have a problem getting it. Nobody else wants it."

Josh walked out of the adobe to where he had tied General and Windy. He decided to ride around town and give it a good look for he would need to know every inch of it if he got the job, and he might just catch a glimpse of Melissa. The adobe buildings were spread over a wide area and they were inhabited by both Mexicans and Americans. The gun store was half adobe and half wood and owned by a middle aged man Josh found to be well versed with the tools of his trade and when asked about the availability of ammunition his weapons used was told plenty was always on hand.

Josh had been told the adobes stayed warm in the winter and cool in the summer and the only fault he could find with them was the size of the door. The doors were short and required his stooping to enter. By their number alone, he found adobes to be the buildings of choice for they outnumbered wood constructed buildings five to one. As he familiarized himself with the businesses of the town, he found no sign of a store bearing the Ryon name.

Melissa had been no where to be seen and Josh began to wonder if the Ryon business was one that was out of town or at their ranch. He hadn't found her yet, but if she was in this town, he would. As he continued his search he saw two young white men heading for a saloon, but more interested in keeping a sharp eye on the bank. Josh rode toward them and when he was close enough to talk to them, he said, "I see you boys are keeping an eye on the bank. Need to make a deposit, do ya? My names Tidwell, Joshua Tidwell. How 'bout us going into the saloon for a drink and leave the bank alone." With those words the two riders wheeled their horses in the opposite direction and headed out of town. He hadn't got the job yet and already he had stopped a bank robbery.

Josh stooped to get through the door of the adobe building that housed the town hall. Upon entry he found himself facing seven men, men he immediately thought made up the town council. The leader of the group walked toward Josh and extended his hand. "I'm Leon Townsend, president of the town council. These gentlemen are the town council," he said and pointed to the men standing behind the two of them. "Mr. Dirksen, our town clerk, has told us that you are interested in the sheriff's position we have open here. Is that true?"

The councilman's hand was small but Josh shook it firmly as he answered the mans question. "Yes, I'm not just interested in the open position, sir, I want the job. Traveled here from Lincoln just for that purpose, and to look up an old friend. Anyone here know a family with the name of Ryon?"

"Well, sir, the job is yours," he said and reached into his pocket and pulled out the bronze badge that read sheriff. "Your reputation has proceeded you and we are pleased that you will be our new authority in town. The job plays forty dollars a month plus board and keep. You pay for your own ammunition."

"Fair enough," Josh said and handed Mr. Townsend a paper with prices written on it. "This paper will let you know what the fines will be for specific offenses that are committed. When the fines are paid, the offender will be released. If the cash is not available to pay the fine, a work detail will set up and the offender will work cleaning up the town until he has worked sufficient time to cover the amount of the fine. Does that sound fair? The town will get two thirds of the fine and I will get one third of the fine. I think that will pay for my ammunition." He smiled a big smile and loved the shock he saw in the faces of the town council. "I don't play favorites in doing my job, so if you don't want to go to jail, don't break the law," he said as he turned and walked from the adobe.

The president of the council was dressed in a brown suit with a red vest. When he had been told the new sheriff played no favorites, his face turned as red as his vest. He was president of the town council and how could this young upstart think he could talk to him in such a manner. He hoped their relationship would not continue to be as rocky as it started.

Josh walked General and Windy to the livery stable and told the young Mexican boy running it that he was the new sheriff of the town and needed two stalls for his horses for which the town would pay.

"Si, senor. The very best for our new sheriff," he said and took Windy and led her to a fresh stall.

"I will use one horse a day and the one not being used I want turned out and exercised."

"Si, senor. It shall be as you ask."

Josh liked the young Mexican. His white shirt and pants were dirty and evidence that he was a good worker and his torn straw hat covered more hair than he had removed back in Little Rock. As he left the livery, he took a coin from his pocket and flipped it to the boy. "You take good care of my horses and there will be more extra money for you, boy. They're easy keepers and your job should be easy, just make sure you do it."

"Si, senor. I will do my best."

Chapter Seven
Albuquerque House Cleaning

Word spread quickly of the new sheriff in town. The last peace officer had been shot in the back and this fact only heightened Josh's senses. Nothing went unnoticed as he walked patrol around the adobes, through the businesses and down the main road as far as the river. There always seemed to be a breeze by the Rio Grande and he liked to walk there to breathe in the fresh air. It was there his first real encounter took place.

The sound of multiple hoofbeats hitting the ground at a rapid pace let him know that more than one rider was loping toward him. As he turned, he recognized the two he had run out of town the first day he arrived in Albuquerque, them and one extra. They had found another fool to join in their race to death and as they closed, Josh pulled the Navy Colt. He called for them to stop and received no response. He called out again and with no response to his second warning, took aim and fired. The ground around Josh exploded as bullets dug into the ground. The first shot had dropped one of the men and his second hit another in the shoulder and knocked him from his horse. The third man turned and tried to get away, but Josh managed to catch a riderless horse and within minutes had the third man in custody. He thought it was better to stop and be arrested than to resist and be buried. Together, Josh and the third rider slowly rode back to collect the shoulder wounded man and the dead shooter. Josh loaded the dead man and the wounded man on the third horse he had gathered up and together they rode to the sheriff's office and to jail. The account set up for fines was really going to grow if these two were ever to see freedom again. That or town would end up the cleanest it had ever been.

Josh had been in town for four days before he saw Melissa. She was driving into town on a buckboard and pulled to a stop in front of the general store. Josh walked to the store and as he entered heard his name.

"Mr. Tidwell is it? Josh Tidwell?

"It is, Mrs. Ryon. You look as lovely as ever," Josh said in a low voice. "It's been a long time since Texarkana, but time seems to have been good to you." He wanted to scream at her for not telling him she was married, but knew the problem was with him. She had done nothing to cause his feelings for they had been conjured up in his own mind. But his unseen rage quieted and he again was the gentleman his father had taught him to be. "Your husband, ma'am. How's your husband? I thought I might see him in one of the businesses here in town. I saw the Ryon building in Fort Worth and just assumed he would do the same here." As she began to answer his question, Josh noted that she was still the beauty he had first encountered in Little Rock.

"We have a small ranch east of town and Tom is out there. He's been real sick for over a month and the doctor can't figure out what it is that's ailing him. I drive into town for supplies when I can find someone to watch him while I'm gone."

"Why not move into town? Wouldn't it be more convenient if ya were closer to the doctor and supplies? Seems to me it would save ya a lot of time and effort. Your place will still be there when your husband gets well."

"We've thought of doing just that, but haven't got around to it."

"When ya decide to move, ya let me know. I'll get ya all the help ya need."

She laughed and said, "I imagine you can. Town seems a lot cleaner and I hear you have an account with the town that has some pretty hefty fines in it."

"Bad guys got ta pay," he said with a big smile. "The disorderly drunk pays a little and the would be murderer pays a lot. I arrested one town councilman for drunk in public and made him pay double to get out of jail. He was supposed to set and example, and the example he set was unacceptable."

The two continued to talk as she shopped and Josh carried her goods to the buckboard as she was leaving. "Hope your husband gets better soon," Josh said as he helped her to the seat.

"Thank you, Sheriff Tidwell. I appreciate that."

"Josh, call me Josh," he added as she drove away.

The drunks kept the account for fines flush and Josh dipped into it regularly to purchase ammunition for he practiced daily. He started carrying a second Navy Colt, but it was unseen as it was carried in a shoulder holster beneath his left arm and shoulder. The holster itself was of Josh's own design. The holster was open to the front of his body. A piece of spring steel had been formed around the the top of the holster and held the sides of the holster tightly together, and the bottom three inches had been stitched together tightly. The end of the barrel sat in the bottom of the holster and the top was spread to insert the weapon and hold it in place. Josh was able, with practice, to draw it from beneath his coat almost as fast as he could draw from his hip. Some had tried to beat the draw from the shoulder holster and some had died. Those that didn't die contributed heavily to the account for fines for attempted murder was the toughest fine of all.

He had even begun to practice with the Henry rifle and did so often from both Windy's and General's back. He still carried two calibers of ammunition for there was no way he would give up the colts. The area where he practiced with the rifle was covered with cactus, beaver tail cactus, and each showed proof of the number of shots he had fired from the Henry. He kept his guns and his ability to use them in perfect shape for his life depended on them.

It seemed that months had passed since Melissa had been to town and Josh wondered if her husband had taken a turn for the worse. He decided to stop by the doctor's place and find out what was going on for himself. Doc Franklin was a man in his late thirties and everyone in town loved the man. He often joked with Josh saying he wished he could get his patients to pay their bills the way Josh got his people to pay into the fines account. This day he wore a long face and said he thought he had found the cause of the sickness of the people to the east of town. "It's in the water," he said shaking his head. "We've got to find the cause of the bad water. Think you can give me a hand?" the Doc asked.

"You bet, Doc. I can leave in the morning, so I'll tell the town council I'm givin' you a hand today. Tomorrow's soon enough, isn't it, Doc? How is Tom Ryon doin'. I haven't seen his wife come to town for supplies lately so I thought I'd find out from you."

"Not good, Josh. I think he's one of the one's effected by the bad water."

"Why not move 'em all to town? The water here is good and there's plenty of it. Let's bring 'em to town."

"A good idea, but they'd bring the sickness with them and we surely don't need the whole town down sick. Let's just try to clean up the water."

The following morning, Josh was up early and walked to the livery stable for General and Windy. He had changed his manner of dress and instead of his black coat and trousers wore a blue shirt with a star on the pocket, tan trousers, and his cavalry boots. He made sure the brown vest he wore allowed his badge of authority to be seen clearly and thought of moving it from his shirt to the vest. His Navy Colts were on his right hip and beneath his left arm and he was ready for the day, no matter what came his way. He stopped by the doctor's home for final instructions.

"I've got some small bottles here for you and I want water samples from everywhere the water surfaces. Mark on the bottles where the water came from and when you get back to town, give them back to me. And be darn careful with the full ones and don't break them. I don't want you sick too. And make sure you carry enough water from town to last until you get back."

Josh took the bottles and walked on to the livery. Manuel had the horses ready and had his bed roll and duster tied to the saddle. Josh watched the boy work and said, "Nice job, son," and flipped him a coin. "I'll be back in a few days." He saw the extra water he had ordered had been secured to the pack rack on Windy's back and with that started from the livery.

"Okay, boss. I'll keep an eye on your place 'til you get back." As Josh rode away, both the doctor and the little Mexican boy, Manuel, watched him until he was gone from sight. The doctor returned to a patient and the Mexican boy to his chores and Josh looked for water as he rode to the east.

As he neared the Ryon ranch he watched for signs of movement for it was still early. He saw the well in the front yard of the home and decided that the Doc had already retrieved a sample of water from it. Seeing no movement in the house, Josh thought they were still sleeping and rode on to the east thinking of the pretty young woman he'd seen in both blue and white and yellow.

The desert was alive with lizards, turtles, horned toads, and snakes. The other variety of life was abundant also. Cactus and sagebrush were plentiful and some kind of orange and blue flowers could be seen scattered across the wide expanse of sand. But he found no sign of surface water.

It was near noon of the following day when Josh found his first sign of water. A small pool was formed between a stand of rocks and Josh filled a small bottle with the liquid. It looked clean enough, but had a strange smell to it. He couldn't place the smell but knew he would recall the scent before he got home. It smelled like some kind of fruit.

Pushing on to the east, the watering holes became more numerous and the fruit smell more pronounced. Near dark, Josh came upon a mining operation and recalled at once the odor that came from the water. It was arsenic.

"Hello in the mining camp," Josh called out. "I'm Sheriff Tidwell from Albuquerque. We need to talk. I'm coming in so don't start shootin'." Josh could see movement in the small shack that had been built close to the mine, but the door didn't open. He called out again and as he did saw the window nearest the door open and a rifle barrel appear.

"Get out of our camp, stranger, and don't come back. Yer gonna find more than ya bargained for here. We'll fight to protect our property."

"I'd come out if I were you 'cause I just found the dynamite ya left by the wood pile and if ya don't come out peaceable like you'll soon be talkin' with the angels.

"We put the dynamite away, friend, so don't try to fool us into thinkin' we'll get blown up if we don't listen to ya."

"I can see y'all are the kind that need showin', so stand clear of the door and window." Josh shoved a fuse into a single stick of dynamite and lit the fuse. He watched the fuse burn and as it shortened threw the stick toward the shack. The explosion that followed knocked Josh from his feet and dazed him. He shook his head to clear it and surmised the miners must have stored their dynamite below the shack for there to have been such a large explosion. The shack was scattered over the desert in small burning pieces as were the men that had lived in it.

Josh was glad that no one had been with him to see the stupid act he had just committed. How ridiculous it had been to use the dynamite. A shot through the window would have served the same purpose and the men in the shack would still be alive. There was no doubt that Josh liked to make a big entrance, but this had gone way to far and he wondered if the men had families that would miss them. It was now dark and he decided to wait until morning to clean up the mess.

As the eastern sky began to lighten, Josh was up and taking care of his horses. He found two old wood boxes and used them to feed the horses their grain. As he looked for the source of the arsenic, he was stunned by the sight of what he had caused the night before. The shack was totally gone and even the floor had disappeared. It had been blown into who knew how many pieces, the largest of which could easily be picked up by hand. Worst of all was the collecting of body parts. He collected all he could find and deposited them in the mine the men had dug into the hillside. He also placed the arsenic and other mining implements in the back of the mine and then lined the opening of the mine with dynamite. The mine in which they worked so hard would be their final resting place, Josh thought as he lit the fuse. He had cut the fuse long enough to allow for him and the horses to reach a safe distance before the blast occurred. The blast that resulted was bright red, yellow and white and brought the hillside down and removed all signs of the existence of the mine.

Josh looked around one last time and was sure that he had cleaned the area well. He drained the pond away from the small stream that kept it full and rerouted the water away from the pond. The cause of the sickness in Albuquerque had been found and cleaned up. Now it would just take time to wash the arsenic from the ground water that flowed to the west and furnished the ranches east of the city.

The trail back to Albuquerque was long and as he neared the city and passed the Ryon ranch he noticed two graves he hadn't seen before. He knew Tom had been sick for a long time and thought he could have been the reason for one, but who could the second have been for? Melissa had not been sick the last time he saw her. He resigned himself to the fact he wouldn't get answers to his questions until he got back to his office.

Manuel was watching the road in anticipation of his friends return. As Josh came into his view, he ran to meet the white man that treated him so well. Out of breath from running, he struggled to talk.

"Mr. Tidwell. Mr. Tidwell, I'm so glad that you are home. The men are in the square and are arguing with the town council. I think you should be there before they get into a fight."

"What are they fighting about?"

"I don't know, Mr. Tidwell. I heard something about city taxes, but I really don't know."

"Thank you, Manuel," Josh said as he reached down and pulled the boy up and behind him on General. As they passed the livery, Manuel slid from the back of the horse and grabbed Windy's lead rope. He led her to her stall and then went back to his chores. He knew his friend would settle the trouble in the square.

Josh tied General to the hitching rail in front of the town hall. He stood quietly and listened to the heated arguing that came from the square. He walked slowly toward the gathering of towns people and listened carefully to what was being said. The town council wanted to raise taxes on the businesses in the city and the money was to be used to raise the sheriff's wages and hire a deputy to share the work of his office. Josh laughed out loud and walked into the crowd.

"Now listen up, folks. To the council I say thank you for the thought, but you know as well as I do that my wages have come from the account set up for fines and the town has yet to spend one dime on my wages. I have collected my wages from fines. To the rest of you folks I say I need no deputy. I can handle my job and don't need help. He looked back at the president of the town council and asked, "Now come on Leon. What's the money really for? You guys are just like the federal government. You tell the people one thing and do another. You collect money for one thing and spend it on another. No one ever knows what you are really up to and the people in town don't like it. Better be honest with the people or you're goin' to get voted out of office."

With those words the crowd began to break up and Leon Townsend thanked Josh for breaking up what was just about to be an unruly crowd.

"I meant what I said, Leon. Better treat the town with honesty or you'll find yourself out of a job. You've got the people pretty stirred up and if you're not careful you're gonna have another Fort Worth. All the good people will leave and you'll be left with those who constantly pay fines into our account. But you won't have anyone to collect 'em, 'cause I'd leave too." He shook his head realizing he was talking to a wall, turned and walked back to the street where General was tied.

"Hey, Doc. Found the cause of your bad water. It's arsenic," Josh said as he rode to the livery and saw the doctor. "Got those samples of water you wanted and I'll bring 'em by your office. Saw two graves out at Ryon's place. Did he die?"

The doctor nodded his head in affirmation and added, "So did Melissa. She was sick before you left and when Tom died, she killed herself. Guess she didn't want to go through the pain she knew her husband had endured prior to his death."

The words the doctor spoke almost tore Josh's heart from his chest and he slumped in the saddle. "I'll bring the water samples by your office and let you know what I found and what I did to correct it." He rode slowly to the livery stable and Manuel was right there to take the horse and lead him to his stall. Josh took his saddle bags and threw them over his shoulder and started back to the doctors home.

It took longer than Josh had expected to explain to the doctor how he had blown up the miners and destroyed the entire outside area around the mine. Especially since he had to do it in a manner that didn't make him look like an idiot. It had been an accident and that was all there was to it.

When he had finished his explanation, the doctors only question had been, "How can you call throwing a stick of dynamite at a building and watching it blow up an accident?" He shook his head and examined the bottles of water Josh had collected. He took them to what he called his laboratory and a few minutes later returned saying Josh was right. It was arsenic. The miner had probably been mining for silver.

"Think those miners could have had relatives in the area?" the doctor asked. "Or maybe other miners that were looking elsewhere for a place to dig when you blew up their friends? Or maybe someone staked them for a piece of the profits and is looking for them now. Think that's possible?" The doctor was having fun at Josh's expense and enjoying every minute of it. He didn't know how close to the truth he really was for three weeks.

Four men rode into town on what Doc Franklin thought to be a Thursday and it could be easily seen that they were heavily armed. They stopped at the town hall and one walked in and in a moment came out with Mr. Dirksen, the city clerk, held by the collar. The clerk pointed toward the sheriff's office and then was released and the man remounted his horse. The four rode toward the adobe the clerk had said was Josh's office.

All four men wore tan colored dusters, but they're hats were of different colors. The taller of the men in the saddles wore a black felt with a flat brim. Next to him was a grey felt with the front and back of the brim turned down. The other two wore a brown, wide brimmed felt that was well worn and the other a brown derby. No one wore a derby in the sun in the middle of the desert, the Doc thought.

The taller of the riders asked the doctor if he had seen the sheriff and wanted to know his name.

"Haven't seen him yet today, but his name is Tidwell, Joshua Tidwell."

"From down around Fort Worth, that Tidwell?" the man wearing the derby asked as he opened his duster and pulled his pistol from its holster. "This is going to be a lot of fun, boss. I've always wanted to go up against a town tamer." Beneath his duster was a faded red shirt and dark brown trousers that looked as if they had needed laundering for quite some time.

It was the tall rider wearing the black felt that answered to boss and when he began to talk, all the riders listened carefully.

"I've seen this kid in action in Fort Worth. He's fast and he's smart and he'll do just what you think he won't. Keep your eyes open and watch his every move or you're going to end up dead. We'll spread out here around his office and wait."

"What do you need with the sheriff?" the doctor asked.

"We're missing some of our people that were supposed to be working a mine about two days east of here. Thought the sheriff might have heard something about them or maybe he saw them. One was my brother."

"Mornin' men," Josh said from behind them. "Mornin', Doc. What can I do for you men?"

"You the sheriff here, the one they call Josh Tidwell?"

"I am, but I don't seem to recognize any of you so you can't be from around these parts. I know every one from here abouts."

"We come from Amarillo and we're lookin' for our friends that worked a mine east of here," the man wearing the black hat said.

"They're dead," Josh said. "Killed in an explosion at their camp. I'm the one that buried all the pieces I could find. And I'm the one that found them dumping arsenic into the stream that flows to all the ranches east of town. They poisoned the water and killed three families that lived out there. I'm also the one that buried the arsenic in the mine and then sealed it up forever. I used the last of the dynamite to seal the mine."

"What caused the explosion?" one of the riders asked.

"I did. They stuck a rifle out the window in my direction so I told them again who I was and told them to come out and without the rifle. They didn't believe me, I guess, and refused to come out. I picked up a stick of dynamite and told them if they didn't come out I'd light the fuse and throw it their way. They didn't come out, so I threw it. I had no idea they stored the rest of the dynamite under the shack, but they did. You know the rest."

"Guess we've ridden a long way for nothing, boys. Let's get started back to Amarillo. We've plenty of provisions and lots of daylight left, so let's get going."

As they turned and rode away, Josh could hear them talking but not what they were saying. He sensed something was wrong. As he started to remove his coat he told the Doc to get off the street for the men were about to return with their pistols in hand.

The man in the black hat yelled, "Now."

All four men wheeled their horses around and drew their guns and charged Josh as he stood in the street by himself. There was something about the man in the derby hat that Josh didn't like so he took aim at him first. As he started to pull the trigger, he dropped to the side of his horse. Josh adjusted his aim, fired and dropped the man from his horse. One down and three to go.

The man in the black hat was next on his list and as he took aim felt the bullet from the mans gun hit him hard in the right side and the an-other in the left thigh. He dropped to the ground and fired twice. Three shots left. He fired again and the third bullet hit its mark and the mans black hat fell to the ground and he landed on it a moment later. Two shots left. The rider in the grey hat was closest and seemed the next logical target. Josh rolled to the water trough next to the hitching post and as the rider passed his position aimed and shot the man in the side at an angle up toward his heart. Seeing the third man fall, the man in the worn wide brimmed brown hat turned and rode out of town. One bul-let left. It was a good thing he carried a second colt beneath his left arm.

As the doctor ran to Josh's side and checked his wounds, Josh said, "First time for everything, huh, Doc. First time I've needed you for bullet wounds."

Maybe so, but this one's the real thing. You're going to be laid up for quite a spell."

Josh wanted to go after the man in the worn brown hat, for he knew that sooner or later he would be back with friends and they would try to kill him again. Now it was Josh's turn to keep watch over his shoulder.

"Sheriff, lay still until I can get some help to get you in the house. I've got to get these bullets out of you." The whole town was watching what had just taken place, but it was Manuel that helped get Josh to the doctors office, a boy doing a mans job.

Chapter Eight

Bonnie Davis

M anuel was the constant visitor to Josh's house as he healed from the bullet wounds and Doc's surgery. No one from the town council had stopped to check on his well being. As the days and weeks passed, the Mexican boy and Josh would walk around town to rebuild his strength. He always carried the Navy Colt and constantly pulled it from the holster, slowly at first and then with each pull that followed added more speed. They were passing the town hall when they noticed the approaching wagon from the south. Josh couldn't see the driver clearly, but noticed he was a small man and not someone sent from Amarillo to take the sheriff's life. They turned and walked back toward the doctors house.

"Excuse me, sir. Your name wouldn't be Joshua Tidwell would it? I'm......

"You're Bonnie Davis," Josh interrupted. "And what the heck are you doing in Albuquerque?"

"You wouldn't come home to see me, so I decided to come see you before you get yourself killed. I take it you've been in a gun fight."

"Yes," Josh replied. How'd you know? Word couldn't have gotten to Lincoln this soon."

"No, it hasn't. But something had to cause the blood on your shirt. You're bleeding again. Get on the wagon and tell me where the doctor lives."

"Manuel, go find Doc. Tell him I need some more stitches." Josh checked his wound as the boy ran for the doctor. "Guess I over did it a touch," he said as he climbed on the wagon. "I know you won't believe me, but it is good to see you Bonnie."

She smiled and answered, "That's the nicest thing you've said to me since we were kids. Now where does the doctor have his office, and where do you live? I'm moving in. Someone has to take care of you and it might as well be me."

Josh could see that Bonnie had changed. She was no longer the young girl that followed him around when she was a child. She was a woman now. He had always thought she was a pretty girl, but now she was a beautiful woman and he knew that as long as she was in town his job was going to be much tougher. He thought the Doc would really like Bonnie for her smile was infectious and she talked all the time.

She moved in and in no time Josh was up and as good as ever. The Doc and her really got along well together and she helped out around his office daily. But as it had always been, Josh was her man. She had loved him when she was a child and had made his life miserable by following him around all the time. And she loved him now and wasn't going to leave his side again until she was sure that he knew it.

Josh too liked the fact that she was living with him and when she announced she was moving out, Josh thought he'd done something wrong. When he asked her what he'd done to cause her to want to move out, she replied "Nothing." This really confused the sheriff.

"You're well now, Josh, and we're not married. Just what do you think the towns people are thinking?"

"Who cares what they think?"

"I do, Josh. If you want me back in here with you, you're going to have to ask me and you know what I mean."

Josh nodded and that afternoon she moved into a small apartment close to the livery stable. She kept him fed and she kept his clothes clean, but she wouldn't move back in with him. She had him hooked now and it was only a matter of time before he would give in.

While passing the mission which was on the route he walked as he kept an eye on the town the Padre appeared in the door of the church. He waved to Josh and said something he didn't understand.

He didn't care 'cause the Padre wasn't on his good list today. Bonnie went to church regularly and it was probably the priest that told her she should move from his home. He shook his head and went on about his business

"Bonnie," the Doc asked, "Are you good with numbers? They're looking for someone to work in the new bank that's good with numbers. When I found out, I thought of you. If you're going to remain in town for a spell, you might as well get a job that pays you. I appreciate your help here, but you know I can't pay you. I barely make any money myself."

"That's okay, Doc, and I appreciate your thinking of me for the job. I really don't need any money though because Josh takes good care of me."

"You truly love him, don't you?"

"I have since we were children, Doc. I thought I lost him in the war when his parents stopped hearing from him, but he finally came home to me. When he left again and came here, I followed. I just can't get him out of my mind."

"Don't tell me no one else has tried to take his place because I won't believe it."

"Sure they have and the most persistent came from Josh's own home. His parents took in this kid named Ted Summers and he did a good job for them. He made it a lot easier on old man Tidwell, Josh's father. I went over to their house one day to see if they had heard from Josh and they introduced me to Ted. He was so funny. He couldn't talk and he couldn't look me in the eye at that first meeting. But that quickly changed. He's been after me every since that first meeting."

"But it's Josh that you're after?"

"Yep. I just can't get over him."

Josh walking into the room quickly changed the topic of conversation and both Bonnie and the Doc smiled at each other as they greeted him. The drunks and the law breakers over the passed month had been especially busy and had added greatly to the account holding the fines collected for providing release from incarceration. As he sat down on a box in the Doc's office he said, "Want to go get some dinner? The fines have been good and I can't think of anyone I'd rather buy dinner for than the two of you. Want to eat?"

"I can eat," Bonnie answered and, looking at the doctor, saw that he was in agreement. "Where we going to eat?"

"You choose, Bonnie. I know you must have a favorite place to eat you haven't told me about."

"We'll go to Doc's favorite. I like it too and the dinners are real good."

When Josh saw where they were headed, he was relieved to see the family dog out front of the restaurant to greet them. It would allow his dinner go down a lot easier. He held the door open for them to enter and as he walked in, he noticed two riders approaching from the south, riders he didn't recognize.

The inside of the restaurant was neat and clean and murals were painted on the walls. One depicted a bull fighter preparing for the final kill in the bull ring. Another was of a Texas longhorn bull, and yet another a portrait of a Mexican gentleman he'd not seen before. The artist was very talented for the paintings on the walls were very good.

As they sat at a table, a young girl approached the table and Doc said, "Hello, Maria. Have you got something good for us to eat today?"

Maria smiled at the Doc for he was one of her regular customers and said, "Enchiladas, tamales, chorizo, beans, chiles, chicken, pork, or steak. Take your pick," she said.

Each ordered their favorite dish and as they ate, the beer and the conversation flowed. Josh sat at the table with his back to the wall and he had a clear view of the entire room. Bonnie sat to his right and the Doc to his left. He expected the riders he had seen earlier to make an entrance shortly and it was important to Josh that he know exactly where everyone in the restaurant was located. To the left and right of their table the way was clear for him to leave if there were trouble and he would move quickly to keep Doc and Bonnie from danger.

The dishes had been cleared from the table and the three friends sat and talked as they finished their drinks when the two men entered the restaurant. They had removed their coats and it was evident they were not there to eat. The taller of the two wore a green shirt, black pants, a grey felt hat and what looked like a colt hung low on his right hip. The other was a Mexican in gaucho attire and wore a large sombrero and carried a shotgun as well as a handgun.

"Joshua Tidwell, is there a Joshua Tidwell here?" the big man asked.

"Don't move 'til I get away from the table, then run," Josh whispered as he got up from the table. "What do you want with him? Is he a friend?"

"Yeah," he said laughingly. "I'm his best friend and I'm here to see he never leaves Albuquerque again."

"I'm Tidwell," Josh said as he saw his friends moving to safety. "I don't want to have to kill you gentlemen, so if you'll place your guns on that table in front of you, I'll try not too."

Josh saw it in the mans eyes. He was going to fight. As the big man went for his pistol, the Mexican's shotgun fired and the chair where Josh had stood exploded. As he dove for the floor, the big mans pistol fired and the bullet smashed into the wall above his shoulder. When Josh finally fired his bullet hit the Mexican in the leg and he hit the floor. He fired again and hit the man in the head and took him out of the fight. Four shots left.

The big man had done this before and as Josh had done, dove for cover. Josh motioned for Doc and Bonnie to use the back door and get out of the restaurant. They disappeared. Josh saw the big mans foot protruding from the table he had upended and used for cover. He fired and saw the man retract his foot, but heard nothing other than the sound of his shot. Three shots left.

"Who are you and what have you got against me?" Josh asked the man who was shooting at him.

"Yancy Baird, sheriff, and I've got nothing against you. You're just a job. No hard feelings, huh sheriff."

"Yancy Baird the gun fighter? I heard you were down in Louisiana workin' as a body guard for some big gambler."

"I still work for him. Who do you think sent me here for you. You killed his brothers. As I heard it you blew one up at his mine and the other killed here in town in a gunfight. That right?"

"Close. The part about the mine is right, but the shooting in town, no. You forgot to add that he came after me with four guns. I take it the one I let go is the reason you're here."

As they talked, both men were trying to position themselves for a killing shot. Josh worked himself to the right and upended a table and then worked back to the left. He remained quiet and listened for some sign of the mans location. A glass fell to the floor and broke and Josh fought and resisted the temptation to fire and move in that direction.

Josh began to tire of the game the two men played and watched the room as best he could from his position on the floor. Then he saw him. His reflection appeared in the window to the left of the door and he was working his way to the left. He had fallen for the upset table Josh had caused. He waited for the man to reach an opening where he could get a good shot. But it was not to happen.

"Let's settle this like men, sheriff. Holster your gun and we'll both stand and fight it out from there. Sound good? How about it? Let's end this."

Both rose from the floor at the same time and both still had their pistols in their hands. Ever so slowly they slid their guns back into their holsters. Josh said, "whenever you're ready."

It sounded as if only a single shot had been fired. Even Josh couldn't remember ever drawing his gun so fast before. Yancy Baird had really been fast, but he would draw no more for the bullet from the Navy

Colt had hit in the center of the chest. Bonnie was the one to see that Josh had been hit too, for he bled from his right side this time and it was only a flesh wound and nothing serious "You're bleeding again, Josh. You sure are hard on shirts. It's a good thing you don't mind wearing patched clothing, 'cause you don't have a shirt that isn't patched." She pulled him close and hugged him. "Don't you ever get scared when you face men like these?" She talked to keep herself from crying and she shook with fear for Josh's life.

"They are the reason I spend so much money on ammunition and the reason I practice so much. That's the only thing that keeps me safe, knowing I'm better than they are in a gunfight." That said, the three-some walked out of the restaurant and to the doctors office.

As he left the restaurant, Josh said, "Check their pockets, Maria. Keep enough money to repair the restaurant and pay for our meals and turn the rest in at my office." The following day he found four hundred seventy dollars on his desk.

The next few weeks went by without even the arrest of a drunk. The city was getting tamed and Josh knew it. Before long the town fathers would be asking him to leave for it was his reputation with a gun that now drew trouble to the town. Until they came for him, he decided to enjoy life and spend as much time with his friends as possible.

Early one afternoon he stopped by Bonnie's house to see if she wanted to accompany him on a ride to his Henry rifle practice range. He didn't knock and just walked in.

"Who's there?" Bonnie called.

"It's Josh," he answered and he saw her through the crack in the open bedroom door. She sat on the edge of her bed and hadn't dressed yet and he couldn't take his eyes from her. She was beautiful.

"Josh Tidwell, can you see me?"

"Yes."

"Do you like what you see?" she asked in a soft voice.

"Yes."

"Then come in."

Josh never did ask her if she wanted to go for a ride, but the afternoon turned to evening and their actions spoke much more than words. The next morning Josh asked Bonnie what she thought the town folks were thinking, but she said nothing and just smiled.

Manuel was raking the livery as Josh arrived to pick up his horses.

He saddled General and when leaving, turned Windy loose to roam. As Josh and the General rode east to the practice area, Windy followed along without the need of a halter and lead rope. The firing of the Henry no longer bothered Windy and Josh taught her to lie down on the ground and allow herself to be used as a platform from which Josh fired the rifle. He laughed to himself as he recalled the first time he had tried it with Windy. It surely wasn't pretty and he still carried the scars on his legs to prove it. She had tried to run over him.

The report of the Henry was loud and Josh didn't see or hear Manuel ride up behind him. When he did see the boy he asked what he was doing so far from town.

"They want to see you, Mr. Tidwell. The town council wants to see you."

"Thank you, Manuel. Let me get off a couple more shots with the Henry and then we'll leave for town, okay?" He took his time lining up his target and even longer to squeeze off the shot. What was waiting for him in town was something he was in no hurry to receive. No one likes to be told they are no longer needed even when the job they performed was what brought about their demise. Manuel and Josh talked as they rode back to town and Josh found out the small Mexican boy was really sweet on Bonnie. "She is so nice to me and she always smells so good, Mr. Tidwell. I think she is the prettiest girl I know."

"Me too, Manuel. Me too."

The two riders were met as soon as they reached the town limits and everyone they passed sounded the alarm set off by the town council. They all knew that Josh was to be let go from his position as sheriff, but no one would tell him that straight out.

Manuel stopped at the livery stable and Josh rode on to the town hall by himself. At the hitching rail in front of the hall Josh slowly climbed from Generals back. He turned to the pinto, Windy, and told her to stay put until he returned. He gave General a couple of good pats to the neck and then walked slowly to the town hall. He ducked as he entered the door and when he looked up found himself facing the entire town council. Leon Townsend, president of the council was the one who spoke.

"Sheriff Tidwell, I am sure you are aware as are we that the town of Albuquerque has been cleaned up and the residents and those who live in the surrounding area have learned that laws are to be kept and not broken.

The account held open in the bank for fines has amassed quite a total. However, the last deposit was made nearly a month ago. It in itself is proof that your manner of cleaning up a town works, and for that we owe you our thanks. It also lets us know that your manner of keeping the law is no longer required. Because of the job you have done, the town council has decided that the entire amount in the fines account should be given you as a bonus. It is a tidy sum, nearly ten thousand dollars. I'm sure you can live on such an amount until you are able to find another job. We thank you again for your services." With those words, he was handed an envelop full of money, and a hand was extended for him to shake. He did, then turned and walked away toward his home and Bonnie without saying a single word. He was only twenty-seven years old and demanded the respect of all with whom he came in contact, but he had no power over the council. There word was final and he would leave, and as he looked down the street and saw Bonnie, knew he would leave with the best looking girl in town.

"Bonnie, do you love me?" Josh asked as he neared his home. "If ya do I have a question I wanna ask ya."

Bonnie stood in front of his home and had witnessed what had transpired up the street as had all the other residents that were milling around in the street. "You know I love you as I always have. Why?"

"Will you marry me?" he asked as he took her hand and pulled her to him. "I want to marry you right now."

"Have I got time to put on a dress?" she asked jokingly. "I have a nice white dress." She hugged him tightly and continued, "Give me twenty minutes and we'll go to the church."

"Done." He called to Manual as he looked toward the livery stable. "Get the Doc and meet me in the mission in twenty minutes."

"You are serious aren't you? You really want to marry me?" Bonnie asked for though this was what she wanted, she had to make sure Josh was serious.

"In twenty minutes at the church or the deals off," he said as he smiled and did everything possible to keep from laughing. He had caught her completely by surprise and for the first time thought he was one step ahead of her.

Thirty minutes later Bonnie Davis was known as Bonnie Davis Tidwell, wife of one Joshua Tidwell, and both were sure their love would last forever. They didn't know what they would do or where they would go, but they were together and right now that was all that mattered. The cantina was their next stop and they brought all their guests, Doc, Father Raphael, and Manuel. There was going to be a party the likes of which Albuquerque had never seen before. A guy didn't get married every day, especially to a woman as beautiful as Bonnie.

Three days later they packed up and loaded the wagon and left Albuquerque for Lincoln. General and Windy were tied to the back of the wagon and as Josh and Bonnie took one last look they saw Doc and Manuel watching them disappear to the south. They would go home for a time and then move on to another town and another job.

"You know something, Josh. I told your mother we'd be married when we returned to Lincoln. And guess what, we are.

Chapter Nine
Lincoln County, New Mexico Territory

J osh and Bonnie back tracked their trip from Lincoln to
Albuquerque, but followed the Rio Grande River south this time
instead of north. They passed colorful pueblos and travelers heading to the north. They watched beautiful sunsets and were ready to
travel again as they watched a magnificent sunrise. They traveled
together and enjoyed each day as if it were their last. The best part
of the relationship was not so much that they loved each other, but
that they liked each other. You can love anyone, Josh thought, but if
you're going to spend twenty-four hours a day with someone, you
really had to like them.

They talked about everything as they rode toward their home in
Lincoln.

Things seen on their trip, her parents, his parents and even children had been discussed. It was when Josh mentioned Ted Summers
that Bonnie got quiet.

"What's the matter, Bonnie? Don't tell me you are tired of talking.
You always have something to say."

"It's Ted. I forgot all about him. He's not going to be very happy
that I married you instead of him."

"I thought he was pretty sweet on you when I was home a while
back. You think he'll be upset, huh. Well, we'll worry 'bout that when
we're confronted with it. I really don't think he should be that much
of a problem."

"All right, but I think we're going to have to be real careful."

"We will," Josh answered as they rode on to the south.

The newly wed couple drove straight through Lincoln and on to Josh's parents home. Seeing them arrive together brought a big smile to his mothers face and seeing the wedding ring on her hand brought tears to her eyes. His father and Ted were with the cattle and didn't know the two had arrived until later that evening.

"Congratulations, son. You got yourself one fine girl. I always hoped one day she'd be part of the family. Have you seen your parents yet, Bonnie?"

"Congratulations, Josh. You got the best girl in town." With those words Ted left the house and wasn't seen the rest of the night.

Liam watched Ted leave the house and knew he was upset, but didn't know why. He knew he liked Bonnie, but had never thought of them together. It was probably better to let him go, he thought and returned to his wife Rebecca's side.

"We didn't stop at my parents place as we came in because they'll have a fit when they find out I married Josh. But I don't care what they think because I know I did the right thing when I married your son."

The merriment and conversation continued late into the evening and when Josh and Bonnie finally made it to Josh's old room the two were arm in arm.

Bonnie whispered in Josh's ear, "Can you see me?"

"Yes," he whispered back. He smiled as he thought that this was the first time he had been with a girl in his room legally.

The days that followed Josh worked with Ted and his father, but the close relationship Josh and Ted experienced before was no more. They hardly spoke for the conversations Josh tried to initiate were met with silence. In his spare time, he and Bonnie were working on the original home built on the homestead. It wasn't far from the main house, but would afford the new couple the privacy they thought they needed. When they moved into the home, Bonnie wanted to be carried across the threshold and Josh obliged. He loved her more than he ever thought he would and his love grew daily. What Bonnie wanted Josh tried to provide. He was thankful that her wants were few and he was able to provide them.

Liam knocked on the door and Bonnie opened it.

"Is Josh here. I need to talk to him about the cattle on the high range."

Bonnie offered him some coffee as he sat at the kitchen table and then went to get her husband.

"What can I do for you, dad," Josh said upon entering the room. "What do the cattle need from me?"

"It's Ted. He's sick and I can't send him up the mountain the way he's feeling. I was wondering if you could work it into your schedule to go up and check on the cattle. In a few weeks we'll bring them down to the lower pastures, but I need to know what's going on now."

"Sure, dad. I'll go up," he said after looking to Bonnie for approval.

"There's nothing happening here that I can't handle myself or with Rebecca's help. You go and I'll keep a candle in the window for you," she said as she smiled at the two men.

It was early October and a light blanket of the winters first snow covered the land just as it had when he left for Albuquerque. General was saddled and Windy carried the supplies they would need for their trip up the mountain. Josh climbed on his horse and with Windy following, rode toward the house. Bonnie came out with some food in a bag that he could eat along the way and his mother handed him a jar containing peach cobbler. She also handed him a fork which she said she wanted back when he returned. He gave them both a kiss and then headed south up the mountain. The women watched as he rode away.

"Bonnie, does Josh know there's no lead line on that pinto?"

"Yes, he does. There's a bond between those three that you just can't explain. You'd have to shoot that mare to keep her from following Josh and the General."

The higher the threesome climbed, the more snow they encountered. Josh saw deer and even some mountain goats as they climbed to the high pastures. The cattle he passed seemed to know that the deep snows of winter were on their way and they were heading north to the lower pasture and warmer weather. One day was gone and another on the way when he got to the high pastures. The night had been cold and the cattle were making their way to warmer places. The General worked cattle well and together, he and Josh pointed the longhorn steers in the right direction and all headed for home.

Bonnie was busy working around the house when the knock on the door came. It was Ted and he didn't seem sick to her at all. He had acted strangely around her since she came back from the north. She hadn't paid too much attention to him before, but now he left her with an uneasy feeling.

"Where are the folks?" she asked.

"They drove into town about twenty minutes ago."

She really felt uneasy now and wished that Ted would leave. "Don't you have work to do?" she asked.

"Sure, but it'll wait. I want to be here with you. We're all alone and no one will ever know what happens here," he said as he watched her inch her way to the door. His eyes betrayed what was on his mind and Bonnie wanted no part of it. As she reached for the door, he grabbed her and carried her to the bedroom and threw her on the bed.

"You're going to be nice to me, real nice to me," he said as he pulled the hem of her dress toward her head.

Bonnie fought him with all of her strength and scratched his face and neck. He tied her hands together and to the head board of the bed. She was still able to kick and did, but he raped her and had his way with her. When he was finished he untied her hands. As he left the room, he smiled and said, "You tell anyone about this and I'll kill you. And don't you worry any 'cause I will be back for more."

Bonnie could do nothing more for she was in shock and was bleeding. She looked to see if Ted was still around and saw him at the barn. She poured fresh water in the wash basin and cleaned herself over and over. It was as if the dirt that had just been forced on her would not wash off. What Josh would do when he found out what happened, she didn't know, but whatever it was would not be enough to pay for what her friend had done to her.

It was hours later that Liam and Rebecca returned home with the supplies they brought from Lincoln. Rebecca collected the goods she had purchased for Bonnie and walked toward her house. She could tell that something important was bothering her daughter-in-law, but didn't say anything about it. She knew if Bonnie wanted her to know she would tell her.

"Have you seen Ted? He needs to help get the supplies in the house and I haven't seen him anywhere."

"No. I haven't seen him all day," she answered without looking at Rebecca.

Rebecca knew Bonnie was lying to her and wondered why she felt she couldn't tell her the truth. She put her arm around Bonnie and asked if there was something she wanted to talk to her about.

"Has Ted done something to upset you, dear?"

"It's not Ted. Really, it's not Ted."

Rebecca now knew that it was Ted that had done something awful to her son's wife and this bothered her. She made up her mind to have Liam have a talk with the boy.

Later Liam found Ted in the barn brushing the buckskin mare he had been given. As he approached the boy he could sense that something bothered him and felt what Rebecca had told him was true. He could see the evidence on Ted's face and neck that he had done something to hurt Bonnie and the old man wanted to know if the boy would have enough grit to own up to it.

"Something is bothering Bonnie, Ted. You've been around here today, you have any idea what it could be?"

"No sir, I wouldn't know anything about that," he said never looking at the man who had given him a home and shelter.

"You sure, son? I can't think of a reason for anyone to want to hurt a person who has never been anything but kind to people. What happened to your face and neck?"

Ted continued to brush his horse and refused to look at Liam. His actions spoke to Liam as sure as the words coming from his mouth would.

"You had your way with her, didn't you Ted? You raped my son's wife and you haven't the backbone to admit the wrong you have done. You should be whipped to within an inch of your life."

Ted spun around, pulled his pistol from the holster and hit Liam in the head knocking him to the ground. He quickly saddled the buckskin and rode away.

Rebecca was still holding Bonnie when she saw Ted ride from the barn. "Liam," she said aloud. "Liam hasn't come out of the barn."

Both women ran to the barn to check on Liam. The sight of his bloody head scared both of them, but his movement and attempt to get to his feet proved he would be okay.

Two days later Josh rode back to the ranch.

Liam never left the house without his hat and when Josh saw him walking toward him with a bandage on his head he couldn't help asking, "What happened old man? Find something harder than a Tidwell head?" He said it as a joke, but seeing no smile appear on his fathers face knew something terrible had happened.

"What is it, dad? Where are Bonnie and mom?"

"Easy, son. They're okay, but you and I have to have a talk."

As they walked to the barn and Josh took care of General and Windy, his father began to tell him what had happened while he was on the mountain. Liam could see that the more he related what had transpired, the more Josh got mad.

Josh ran to the house and as he entered saw Bonnie in tears and his mother consoling her. He took his wife in his arms and said that everything would be okay now for he was home. He held her tight and told her what had happened was not her fault and that he would make sure nothing like this ever happened again. The rest of the day and into evening he reassured her that he loved her and would take care of her forever.

It was after she went to bed that he cornered his father and asked where Ted would have gone.

"There's a young Mexican girl in town he goes to see," his father said.

"Her name is Rosa Cruz, I think. He probably went there."

"Bonnie is sleeping in my old room. Keep and eye on her, will ya dad?

I'll be back as soon as I take care of some business in town."

"Don't go in shootin', son. We don't need anyone else hurt because of what has happened here."

"I promise, dad. There won't be any shootin' in town. I'll hurt him, but I promise I won't shoot him." With those words said, Josh left the house and headed for the barn. He saddled General and rode toward town. Windy raised such a fuss at being left behind that Liam let her out of her stall and she ran down the road to find her friends.

The Cruz home was not hard to find and Josh pounded on the door until it opened.

"I'm looking for Ted Summers," he said to the cute young girl that answered the door. "If he's here, send him out or I'll be comin' in and I don't think you'll like what happens."

"He's gone. He took my sister and rode away about half an hour ago."

"Which way did he go?"

"West. Toward Fort Stanton."

Josh turned back to General and saw that Windy had found them. As he rode to the west, he knew he could really keep pressure on Ted using both horses to chase him. When daylight would come, he would have no trouble tracking Ted for his horse wore a bar shoe on his right foreleg hoof. Josh knew it would only be hours before he caught up with him.

It wasn't noon yet when Josh saw the two riders on a well lathered horse trying to scale a cleared hillside that had provided lumber to build Fort Stanton. The riders were attempting to make the thick pines that were farther up to help disguise their escape. When Ted turned and saw that Josh was in close pursuit, he pushed Rosa from the back of his horse and she hit the ground hard. He spurred the buckskin hard and blood ran his flanks.

Windy had taken Generals place and she was still fresh. The distance between the two men closed ever faster and Josh paused the chase only long enough to see that Rosa was uninjured. Both Ted and Josh topped the hill and were gone from Rosa's sight, but she could hear the screams of a man being tortured and it went on for some time. When it had remained quiet for a time Josh reappeared and helped Rosa to General's back and they rode together back to town. Ted's buckskin had run off when Josh knocked him from the saddle and disappeared from sight.

Two days later it was all over town that a naked man had been found hanging high up in a giant pine tree. Some said it looked as if he'd been castrated. When Josh heard the rumor, he smiled.

Chapter Ten
The Tidwell Ranch

T he years that followed the hanging were good for the Tidwell family. The number of males in the group had increased by one. Master William Tidwell had been the last to come along and he was the spitting image of his father. Grandma Rebecca doted on the boy and spoiled him rotten. Like his father, William, better known as Billy, loved cobbler and most of the time it was ready upon his request. Josh thought it was great for he always got some too.

Billy never had a pony. He wouldn't have it. He had to have a big horse like his dad and both General and Windy had provided him with hours of horsemanship training. At five he could ride like an adult and he felt he was just like his dad when he rode General and Windy followed along with no lead rope. Many times his father had gone to the barn to saddle General only to find his son had already been there and both were gone. On his sixth birthday Billy received his own horse, a tall four year old sorrel gelding he renamed Blaze because of his bald face.

If Billy was not being tutored by his mother or grandmother, you could bet he could be found with his father or grandfather working side by side with them and carrying his share of the work load around the ranch. He would much rather work with the men than waste his time learning from books and in that respect he was just like his father. He was also a loving and devoted son and grandson who would do or try to do anything he was asked and in that respect was more like his mother. He didn't know of his fathers notoriety as a town tamer for he was too young to understand why he had chosen such a career, but he did know of his expertise with a pistol and his old Henry rifle. He had to be ten years old before he would be taught to use a gun, his father had told him. Nearly six now, he constantly reminded Josh of his promise to teach him to shoot in only four more years.

The cattle business was good and the ranch was turning a good profit.

Better yet was the fact that Josh was happy running the ranch with his father and his desires to go town taming hadn't surfaced for some time. The Tidwell Ranch brand was on thousands of head of hereford and Texas longhorn cattle and Billy was like his fathers shadow as they rode among them checking for new calves and sick stock.

The dead man they found near the lower pastures was quite a surprise for Billy and a sad note to Josh. Billy had never seen a dead man before and to Josh's surprise, it didn't bother his son to see the man lying there in the deep grass.

"Billy, are you okay?"

"Sure, pop. I'm just trying to see if I knew him."

"Take Blaze and go back to the barn and have Grandpa get a buckboard ready to go to town."

"Okay, pop." He was on his way as the words he spoke passed his lips.

Josh knew of the of the trouble a man named Murphy was having with Tunstall and McSween and he wanted no part of it. Finding the body on his property changed things for they had brought their fight to his home. Now he would take the body to town and tell them again to keep off his ranch. One dead steer, an injury to anyone in his family or to one of his hands would bring down the full extent of his wrath. Their stupid battle had awakened the town tamer in him and someone would pay for doing so.

The dead body in the back of the buckboard drew little attention. It wasn't the body, but the man driving the rig that caused the people to wonder what the dead man had done for Josh to need to kill him. He continued through town and stopped in front of the two story brown building that housed the sheriff and the city jail. The sheriff, a man named Richard Brewer, came out of the building to meet him.

"Morning. What have you got there in the back?"

"Morning Brewer. Found this body in my low pasture. He was dead when Billy and I found him. Got no idea who he is."

"Anyone could have done it. Just about every day I get involved with another murder. There's two groups here about that've been feuding for a while now. Seems ole Murphy wants to own everything and McSween won't let him."

"What they do is their business. But if it gets someone from my spread hurt or killed, I'll be settling this little war they got goin'."

As they removed the body of the dead man from the back of the buckboard Sheriff Brewer said, "I'll let them know what you said, Josh. I'm sure they won't want to get you involved."

Billy, who had accompanied his father to town, sat quietly on the buckboard seat, but the conversation he had just heard got him to thinking.

As they started back to the ranch, Billy could no longer hold back his questions.

"Pop," he started, "Why are people afraid of you? The way the sheriff was talking to you, I thought you were friends. But he was afraid of what you might do. Why? You never hurt anyone. You help 'em.

"It's a long story about when I was young and you're too young to understand. When you're older I'll explain why people treat me like they do."

"I guess I got to be ten, huh? That's when I get to learn to shoot, so you'll tell me then, huh?"

"We'll see, boy. We'll see."

"Boy I wish I was ten."

The Lincoln County War raged all around them, but the Tidwell's were left alone to raise their cattle. A new hereford bull they had just received from Texas got loose and Josh went after it. As usual Billy was right behind him and as the bull turned to charge, Josh got out of the way and as he passed saw Billy in the bull's path. As the bull neared the boy, he pulled his feet up on the saddle and looked as if he were preparing to jump. He did jump, but not out of the bull's way. He jumped on the bull's back. As if he had been ridden before, the bull settled down, slowed to a walk and Billy rode it back to its pen in the barn. He slid from the bull's back and closed the stall gate. He looked his father in the eye and said, "We better not tell mom or grams about this."

"Why is that," Josh asked.

"You'll get in trouble, pop."

As the years passed, the Tidwell family prospered. There had been lean years, but they overcame them and continued to build their cattle empire. Billy matured into manhood and looked exactly like his father, but disliked being called Billy and had shortened it to Bill. Rebecca was growing old and her hair had turned to grey. It was plain for all to see that her eye sight was failing a bit as she often thought she was talking to Josh and it turned out to be Bill. Her health was still good as was Liam's and they worked around the house and barn daily. Josh had also aged well and only the grey hair above his ears gave away his age. Bonnie was as beautiful as she was the afternoon Josh had first made love with her in Albuquerque and their love for each other was stronger than it had ever been. Life treated them all well and they were grateful.

Bonnie's parents were rarely mentioned in the conversations of the day. They never wanted their daughter to marry Josh and when she did nearly disowned her. Bonnie went by to see them on a regular basis and had often taken Billy so they would know their grandson. She had seen them just two days before they were killed when caught in the middle of a gunfight outside Lincoln. Her sadness tore Josh apart for he knew he was the cause of her parents feeling toward the Tidwell family.

The Davis Ranch bordered the Tidwell Ranch and was also a cattle raising facility. Upon the death of Bonnie's parents, the ranch was willed to her. She was the recipient of a ranch, land, and cattle that made her a very wealthy woman in her own right. It was the town banker, Henry Booker, appearing at the door that let her know just how wealthy she really was.

"Mrs. Tidwell, is Bonnie home? I need to talk to her if it's alright with you," he said as Rebecca opened the door. He was dressed in a dark suit and tie and wore a black derby to keep the sun from his bald head.

"Come in, Mr. Booker. I'll get her for you," she said while thinking he looked more like the undertaker than a banker.

As Bonnie entered the room, Booker stood and waited for Bonnie to sit down before he sat back down himself.

"What can I do for you, Mr. Booker?" Bonnie asked.

"It's not what you can do for me that brings me to your ranch. It's what your parents and I are doing for you."

"And what might that be?"

"You are the owner now of the bank accounts your parents kept in our bank. If I may say so, Bonnie, you've been willed a tidy sum."

"I knew my parents banked with you Mr. Booker, but you know how they felt about me marrying Josh. I have no idea how they managed their business or their bank accounts."

"If you add the accounts together, they total over two hundred thousand dollars. A sum I hope you won't find necessary to remove from the bank. You will need to come by the bank in the next couple of days to change the name on the accounts to yours. And Mr. Wilford, the town attorney, has asked me to have you drop by his office also. He said something about changing the names on the deeds of property."

Bonnie was stunned. She had no idea her parents had such a sum in the bank. As Booker stood up to leave, she said, "Thank you for coming all the way out here Mr. Booker. I'll be in to see you tomorrow."

Bonnie couldn't wait for Josh to return to the house from a day of work and seeing Bill at the barn sent him to bring his father in early. In less than an hour, the two men returned to the barn.

"Better see what mom thinks is so important, pop. I'll take care of the horses." As Josh left the barn Bill was rubbing on Blaze and he thought how he and General had done the same when they were young.

Bonnie met him about half way to the house and gave him a big kiss and hugged him tightly.

"Maybe this can wait until we go to bed tonight, Bonnie.

"That's not the reason I sent for you, you old man. I can remember when it was hard for you to keep your hands off of me." She laughed and said she had good news.

Upon entering the house, they joined Rebecca and Liam at the kitchen table. Bonnie saw she had their attention, so she began to relate to them her visit with Mr. Booker. Both of the men's mouths fell open upon hearing of Bonnie's fortune.

"What are we going to do now," she asked her husband.

"It's up to you, honey. They were your parents and they left it all to you. It's really your decision to make."

"I'm asking what you all think we should do. We are a family and we all should make the decision. It effects us all."

"Your parents ran a good business and all the hired help is still on the ranch. Let's combine the two ranches into one big one and see what happens. We can call a meeting of all the Davis hands and let them know what we are going to do and those that want to stay can and the others can leave. I've had a run in with a couple of the hands and they'll probably want to leave rather than work for us. Later on when Bill is ready we can let him run the spread. It'll be good for him to get some experience having to run a big ranch and learn how much it costs to maintain it."

"It's decided then. We'll merge the ranches."

Liam, Rebecca, Bonnie and Josh were all in agreement.

Bill entered the kitchen and overheard the latter part of the conversation and knew it wasn't what he wanted, not right now anyway. He was ready to venture out into the world and find his own way as his father had done years earlier.

It was at the supper table three weeks later that he announced he was leaving for Amarillo the next morning. His statement stunned his family and it was quiet for just a moment.

"You'll do no such thing," his mother ordered.

"Easy, Bonnie. We knew this was coming. We just talked about it a few days ago. The boy's a man now and has the right to follow his own mind and do what he thinks is necessary," his father said as he lightly touched his wife's shoulder. "He'll be fine."

Tears began to run down his grandmother's face as they did from his mother's. Grandpa Liam put his hand on his grandson's shoulder and said, "I'll miss you, boy. You make sure you stay safe and keep in touch with us. I hate to see you go, but you just remember, I couldn't be more proud of you."

Bonnie covered her face with her hands to hide the fact she was crying. Unable to control her emotions, she left the table and walked from the kitchen.

"Guess I could have picked a better time to tell you, huh dad. I think I ruined everyones supper."

"Your mother will be fine, son. She just wants you to be her little boy forever. You know how mother's are, they have to keep their babies close. You have a good head on your shoulders and you know what's right. You just remember what you've been taught and you'll be fine."

Liam nodded his head in approval of what was said and went back to his meal. He was silent for a moment and then added, "You know, boy, what your father did when he left home. He kept grandma and me wondering if we'd ever see him again when he left for the war. When we heard he got the handle of a town tamer, I thought your grandma would die.

But, she didn't and neither did your father. He packs some terrible scars that tell the story of his life, and if it's all the same to you, I hope you don't follow in his footsteps."

Chapter Eleven
William "Bill" Tidwell

B ill had learned well the lessons of life his father had taught him and he was an accomplished rider, cattleman, and a fair and thinking man. He was also well trained in the art of self defense and marksmanship. He was adept with both a pistol and a rifle. Unlike his father who favored his Navy Colts and Henry rifle, Bill liked the new Colt Peace Maker pistol and the new Winchester rifle that used the same ammunition as his pistol. He never found the need to carry a second pistol and disliked the shoulder holster his father sometimes wore. Often he had drawn his pistol against his father and was yet to have been able to beat him. He often wondered how his father, at his age, could consistently beat him to the draw. He was just glad it had never been done for real for he enjoyed the life he led.

As he saddled Blaze in the barn, he saw his mother making her way out to talk to him. He smiled as she approached and hated being the cause of the way she felt.

"I'm not going to cry again, I'm all cried out," she said to her son as she entered the barn. "But I do want you to remember we're always here for you and you can always count on us for help."

"I know, mom. This is just something I have to do."

"I know. You really are your father's son. He left me when he was twenty-one and now you're leaving me at twenty." She handed him some money and told him to put it in his pocket before his dad came out. "I had to go find your dad to bring him home. Don't you make me do the same with you." She hugged him tightly and then walked with him out of the barn and toward the house with Blaze in tow.

"Thanks for the money, mom, but I don't need it. I have enough of my own. Besides, dad gave me a bunch last night. He said he didn't want me to get my start money the way he got his. He mentioned something about a Union Army major. Do you know what he was talking about? I sure don't."

His grandparents came out of the house, gave him a big hug and wished him a safe journey. His grandma handed him a napkin which she said contained some sandwiches, a couple of cookies and a small jar filled with cobbler.

"There's a fork in there too and I expect you to return it when you come home," Rebecca said as she brushed a tear from her eye.

"Where's dad? I haven't seen him this morning."

"He was up and out early," his grandpa said. "He must have had something important to do because he left in a hurry. Just hold on, he'll be back soon."

General was in a full lather as Josh rode him up to the house and Windy wasn't far behind. He jumped from the saddle and pulled a package from his saddlebags and handed it to Bill. "Just something to remind you of home, son. Hope you like it."

Bill opened the package and found a new Colt Peace Maker pistol with an engraved barrel and inlaid handles that read 'Tidwell'. He felt the heft of the gun, twirled it in his hand and found the balance to be perfect.

"Thanks, dad. I really like it." He pulled his old gun from his holster and shoved it in his saddlebags and replaced it with the new one.

"Don't let it get you in trouble," his father said. "Use it for good and your protection."

The two shook hands, hugged and then Bill climbed on Blaze and disappeared into the pines that lined the road to Lincoln.

Bill had made no plans as to where he might travel. He knew his fathers name was well known in New Mexico and Texas and would be less known in Arizona, Utah, Nevada or California. It had been a long time since his fathers fame had spread throughout the west as a town tamer and he hoped it would not become something he would have to compete with in the future. The closest four states gave him more than enough room to move around and find himself, so he rode to the west and followed the sun and wondered what he would find down the mountain.

It took Bill three days to make it down to the desert floor and he found that the cooling shade provided by the pines was gone and scrub cedars took their place. Sagebrush and cactus he found was plentiful and the deer and fowl of the high country were replaced with ground squirrels, prairie dogs and desert pheasants, better known as road runners. He was amazed that without all the tall pines blocking your view, you could see for miles as the dust being stirred up in the distance proved. He couldn't see what caused it, but the dust had to be two or three miles away.

He was headed for Las Cruces, New Mexico and it would be the city from which he would start his journey. The dust he was watching in the distance grew closer and seemed to be on an intercepting course with him.

He stopped and decided to wait to see who or what it was that was closing on his position. He reached down and pulled his Winchester out and using the lever action, chambered a cartridge. He rested the butt of the rifle on his leg and waited. It was a horse that kicked up the dust, but it had no rider. As it got closer, Bill replaced the rifle in the scabbard and spurred Blaze and in a flash was running beside the lathered horse. He reached for the reins and slowed both the horses to a walk. There was a canteen of water hanging from the saddle horn and a colt pistol in a holster made into the pommel. The gelding seemed well cared for and he thought it strange for such a horse to be running free when fully saddled. Having nothing better to do, he decided to back track the horse and try to find the rider.

It was easy tracking for no other tracks were to be found other than those of the gelding. In just over an hour of easy riding and topping a small rise he was greeted by a cry for help.

"Over here, sir. Look to your left. Please help me."

Bill saw her and headed in her direction. She was in the shade of a thick greasewood bush and he could see she was bleeding from a wound on her right upper arm.

"What are you doing out here in the desert by yourself?" he asked as he checked her arm. There's nothing around for miles."

"Oh, no sir. My home is just over the rise to the west, about three miles from here." She moved her right arm with her left hand and said, "I think my arm is broken."

Bill took a large bandana from his saddlebags and formed a sling for her arm and tied it around her neck. "I think you are right, young lady. It's broke pretty good."

"My moms gonna kill me. I'm not supposed to ride so far from the house."

"I won't tell her if you don't," he said while smiling at her. "I'm Bill Tidwell. Who are you?"

"I'm Mary Parker and I"m eight years old. Nice to meet you and thanks for the help and the return of my horse. He's Bullet. He got that name because he's so fast. A snake spooked him and he threw me."

"Is that right. We better get you home before your mom misses you, okay. We don't want her mad at you." She was a cute young thing and her blond pigtails reached half way down her back. Her straw hat was still on her head and her dress was nearly new, but now coated with dust and dirt.

He picked her up and put her in her saddle, then handed her the reins and told her to ride slow because the jarring was going to hurt her arm. He told her he would follow along and make sure she made it home okay.

Mary's mother met the pair as they closed on the home. The house was a big adobe with a large patio area shaded by large cottonwood trees.

The patio was surrounded with flower beds that were full of mul-ticolored flowers. Bill pulled Mary from her saddle and carried her into the house where her mother checked the break. She left for a moment and then returned with two pieces of wood. She wrapped the boards with cloth, tore long strips of cloth and rolled them and then turned to Bill.

"We have to set her arm. You've got to hold her down tight and I will pull and set the arm. We'll use the padded boards for splints and the rolled cloth to tie the splints in place. Okay. Are you ready?"

Bill nodded and got a good grip on Mary. With the first pull on her arm, Mary screamed and then passed out from the pain.

With her arm set and back in a sling and snuggly tucked into bed, her mother said, "I guess it's about time for me to introduce myself. I'm Tessa Parker, mother of the monster in the bedroom. I want to thank you for finding my daughter and bringing her home. How far out was she?"

"Not far," he said. "I found Bullet first and then I backtracked and found Mary. She's quite a little lady and really likes to talk," he responded with a smile.

"I didn't ask her what happened, did you?"

"It was a snake that spooked Bullet and he threw her."

"She'll be sore for a spell and will wear the splints for a month or so, but she'll be okay. She's tough."

"You tell her father for me that she was a real trooper."

"She has no father. He was killed during a rain storm when his horse broke its leg in a prairie dog hole. He was trying to stop a stam-pede and was trampled to death."

"I'm sorry to hear that," Bill said. "I guess I better get on my way if I'm going to make Las Cruces tonight."

"Nonsense. You'll never make Las Cruces tonight. It's a half day ride from here. You can stay here and leave in the morning. I'll make some dinner in a while and we can eat it on the patio and watch the sun set. I'm going to go check on Mary."

As she got up and walked to her daughters room, Bill watched her closely. She had to be about his age and she looked young and beautiful and happy with her lot in life. Her hair was dark brown and long, but pulled up off of her neck. The long sleeved blue shirt she wore looked like her husbands, but allowed one to see she was definitely a woman, and her dark pants topped black boots. He wondered what she would look like in a party dress. As she disappeared in Mary's room, he wondered how she could have an eight year old daughter.

Bill went outside and looked around the ranch. He walked Blaze to the barn and found Bullet, still saddled, eating some hay. He walked the horse to a stall and removed the bridal and saddle and filled the feeder with fresh hay and gave him fresh water. He put Blaze in the empty stall next to Bullet and gave him a good brushing as he ate. The barn was well equipped with horse equipment as well as farm equipment. Part of the family raised cattle while the other part worked a garden. "Things never change, he thought. We did the same thing at home."

His walk back to the house found Tessa's ranch hands returning to the the bunkhouse and stabling their horses. A large table was being set in front of the bunkhouse and food was being brought out by the women that worked in the kitchen. Thinking this was where he too would eat, made his way toward the long table.

"Bill, over here. Come over to the patio."

Tessa was calling to him and he saw at once that she now wore a dress. As he got to where she was standing, she took his arm and led him to the patio.

"We'll eat here with Mary if she wakes in time for dinner. If she doesn't, it will be just the two of us. Can I offer you a drink? I have wine, whiskey, or beer. Cold beer."

"If you tell me what you are having, I'll get it and a beer."

"One cold beer coming up," Tessa said as she disappeared into the house. She turned to see if Bill was watching her and he was. When she returned she had a beer and a full glass of red wine.

Supper consisted of bits of steak cooked in some sort of chile sauce, rice, beans and of course, tortillas. Several more glasses of wine and beer were also consumed. Small talk had filled the evening, save the time spent in silence to watch a beautiful multicolored sunset. Late in the evening Mary got up and wanted to eat and Tessa took her to the kitchen to heat her supper. Mary brought her plate to the patio and joined in the conversation. When she went back to bed, Bill said, "She's a tough one, that Mary. You know she still has to be in a lot of pain."

"She's her fathers daughter. She acts and talks just like he did. It's getting late and you must be tired. I'll show you to your room."

"Well, thank you. I thought I might be staying in the barn tonight."

"Oh no, you deserve the best. You saved my daughter's life."

Tessa showed Bill to his room and turned down the bed. "Sleep well. I'll see you in the morning."

Bill waited for all the candles and lamps to go out and then slipped out of the house and saddled Blaze. Minutes later he rode toward Las Cruces.

Fifteen minutes later Tessa walked into the room where Bill should have been sleeping.

As he rode south in the direction of Las Cruces he began thinking about his name for it was something he pondered often. He didn't mind having been called Billy when he was young, but now, Bill just didn't sit well with him and it just didn't fit the person he wanted to be. He was unaware of what the future might hold, but he knew Bill wasn't going to be a part of it. He wasn't sure William was appropriate either, so he shortened it to Will. From now on, he decided, he would be known as Will Tidwell.

The moon tried to shine through the clouds as he rode south to Las Cruces and a cool breeze blew softly from the west. As he took in the nights changing sights created by the moving clouds above, he grew tired.

If he were headed home, he could sleep in the saddle for Blaze knew the road home. But here, they were both strangers and where Blaze might wander he didn't know. He stopped at a large cottonwood tree beside a dry creek to spend the remainder of the night. He pulled the saddle from Blazes back and tied him to the tree, and then unrolled his bed roll. As he tried to find a comfortable position to sleep, he felt a lump under his hip. He lifted the bed roll to smooth the dirt beneath it, but found no rocks or mounds of dirt. He reached into the bed roll and felt something and pulled it out. It was an envelop and why he hadn't found it before he didn't know. The envelop he found had writing on it and he strained his eyes and read, "Thought this might help. Remember, we love you. Grandpa". The envelop was stuffed with money and he thought it would be a while before he had to find work for he had received over two thousand dollars from his family.

Morning came quickly and Will knew he had to find water for Blaze and himself. He saddled the gelding and began his search for water as he rode south toward Las Cruces. He quickly learned that water was more scarce than he had been told and decided he would carry more than he actually needed as he crossed the hot dry sands of the southwestern desert. Noon found him entering the city and a steam locomotive belched steam as it slowed to stop at the railway depot.

Las Cruces, he was told by a station attendant, was growing rapidly since the city had granted free easement to the railroad to lay their tracks through the city. The town of Mesilla had been the railroads preferred route through this part of the state, but the city refused to sell the railroad right-of-way easements. Mesilla ended up the looser and Las Cruces received the benefits of increased commerce and a population explosion.

The town itself was busy with people working and others shopping in the stores that were built across from the train station. Will walked Blaze slowly down the main street watching the people, looking at the businesses, and searching for a place to eat. He was starving.

The small cafe was called Murphy's Place and Will stopped to eat. While tying Blaze to the hitching rail and leaving the reins long enough for him to reach the water trough he said, "You're next, old man. When I get finished eating it will be your turn." Will rubbed the neck of his eighteen year old gelding and then walked into the cafe.

"Morning stranger. Haven't seen you around here before. Glad you stopped in. I'm Murphy. What can I get you to eat? You look pretty hungry."

"I'll have some eggs, some bacon, biscuits and gravy and some coffee, please."

Murphy was a good sized man and it was evident he liked his own cooking. As he looked around the cafe he saw the man seated at the counter across from him looking at his gun.

"Tidwell, is it? You related to Joshua Tidwell? I knew him when he was sheriff in Albuquerque."

The man was dressed in a dark suit, white shirt and tie and looked to be a local businessman. He looked to Will to be in his fifties.

"I'm Will Tidwell. Josh is my father."

"I knew it. You look just like you father. I'm Doc Franklin and your father and I were good friends. In fact, I was a guest at your parents wedding, Manuel and I."

"It's nice to meet you, Doc. My father has spoken of you many times and told me how you saved his life after being shot up in a gun fight. If you don't mind my asking, why did you leave Albuquerque?"

"It got to big, son. Too many people, too many gun fights and too much business. Besides, after your dad and Bonnie left, it just wasn't the same. I really missed them and still do."

As Will ate his breakfast, the doctor told him stories of his fathers exploits, some of which he hadn't heard before. When finished eating, the doctor said it was time to see patients and got up to leave. They shook hands and as he opened the door to leave turned to Will and asked, "Does your dad still have that big black stud and the pinto that followed him everywhere he went?" When Will answered yes, he smiled a big smile and said, "I'm glad to hear some things never change. That was some trio." He then left and walked toward his office.

Murphy began clearing the dishes from the table and thought this would be a good day. One of his first customers of the day had been the son of a famous gunfighter and he couldn't wait to tell his regular customers as they came in to eat. Yes, this would be a good day.

Las Cruces didn't have what Will was looking for and so he decided to ride farther west. He wasn't sure what he was looking for, but knew it wasn't here. Nor was it in Deming or Lordsburg. They seemed to be two wide spots in the road the railroad had built for their steam engines to stop and take on enough water and wood to make it to the next town. The only thing the towns had of interest to him was that Deming was where the Southern Pacific and Santa Fe Railroads came together making the second transcontinental railroad tie and Lordsburg was the home of Elizabeth Garrett, the daughter of Pat Garrett, the infamous sheriff that shot and killed Billy the Kid.

Crossing into Arizona went unnoticed for the landscape and wildlife never seemed to change. The greasewood and cactus and the lizards and snakes of New Mexico looked just like the ones in Arizona. Will began to think he had started out in the wrong direction. Wilcox and Benson were much the same as the towns he had seen in southwestern New Mexico and nothing really caught his attention until he saw Tucson. This town really caught his attention.

Tucson was the largest city he had been to since leaving home. The people were mostly friendly and accommodating and Will decided he might stay for a few days. He visited most all of the restaurants in town and had a few drinks in the many saloons. But it was the Butchers Block cafe where he spent a lot of time. Amanda James worked as a waitress there and Will thought she was the prettiest girl he had ever seen. He began eating his supper there in hopes that he might have a chance to walk her home and get to know her better.

Frank Sutton also ate at the Butchers Block and he too was interested in the young waitress. He lived with his parents and his father owned the freight line that distributed goods brought in on the trains to the businesses around town. Will knew this young man had been sent to court Amanda by his father for she was the daughter of the town mayor. All this Will learned by listening to the patrons and to Amanda herself.

Amanda and Will had become good friends and this didn't sit well with Frank Sutton and he told her so. Her answer to his brash and unwanted words was a hard slap in the face which she was sure would leave a bruise. That evening she was escorted home by a tall, sensitive young man from Lincoln, New Mexico. The weeks that followed found the two growing closer and closer. All their free time was spent together. They had fun together and enjoyed each other, until the Sutton's started causing trouble.

It was early in the evening as Will walked Amanda to her front door that he saw Abel Sutton talking to Mayor James. He felt instantly that no good would come from this conversation and Frank Sutton was something less than a man for having his father do his dirty work. He escorted Amanda passed the two men and opened the door for her. As he turned to leave, Amanda's father stopped him and asked, "Is it true that you are the son of Joshua Tidwell, the infamous sheriff from Fort Worth and Albuquerque?"

"Excuse me, sir. I believe you used the wrong word. You should have said famous sheriff rather than infamous sheriff. I think I know the man better than you."

The mayor's face turned beet red hearing the words Will spoke. He seemed to have lost his train of thought and was at a loss for words.

Will continued, "Yes, I am the son of Josh Tidwell. And, yes, he was a sheriff in Fort Worth and Albuquerque. He cleaned up both towns so that descent folks could walk the streets and feel safe in their surroundings. I'm no fool, sir, so don't treat me as one." Will touched the brim of his hat and walked away.

Amanda saw and heard what had taken place and she was proud of Will for standing up to her father. As her father entered the house she looked at him with a scowl on her face and said, "Father, you should be ashamed of yourself. You had no cause to talk to Will the way you did. He is a descent man and I like him. If you and Mr. Sutton think I'll have anything to do with Frank, you are badly mistaken."

Once his anger had subsided and his blood pressure dropped to a safe level, he began to think rationally about what had just taken place. He was mayor of Tucson and two young people, one his own daughter, had given him a severe tongue lashing. He did learn that evening his daughter was no longer his little girl, but a young woman with a mind of her own.

Will got Blaze from the livery stable early the following morning and was thinking of heading out for Tombstone. He was sure the episode with Mayor James had put an end to his access to his daughter so he tied his bedroll to his saddle and rode south out of town. He stopped at the train station long enough to send another telegram to his parents saying he was okay and temporarily in Tucson. As the telegraph operator read over his message, he paused when he saw the name.

"Your name is Tidwell? Will Tidwell?"

Will nodded and said, "Yes, I'm Tidwell."

"You any kin to a Bill Tidwell from Lincoln, New Mexico."

"Yes, I'm him."

"Thought you were Will."

"My full name is William Tidwell. Bill and Will are short versions of William."

"I understand, sir. But you have to understand I can't give a telegram to just anyone."

"I'm not receiving a telegram, I'm sending one."

"You're doing both. You're sending one and I have one for you."

"Give me the telegram, please." How long have you been holding it?"

"Came in this morning I guess. The night man got it off the wire."

The telegram read, "Bill Tidwell. Come home fast. Father shot. Rest of family okay. Serious. Mom."

Send this as soon as possible, it's a family emergency. "On next train east. Home soon. Wire condition to Las Cruces. Bill."

"I'll send it right now, sir. Hope everything turns out okay. Twelve words, one dollar and twenty cents please."

Josh paid for the telegram and two tickets on the train east. One was for him and the other was for Blaze. Then he looked for Amanda.

His ride up the main street toward the Butcher's Block was fast and direct. He knew nothing of the true condition of his father and he was afraid he wouldn't make it home in time to see him while still alive. The telegram had said serious, but how serious and where had he been shot? Was it a stomach wound or had a bullet pierced a lung? He had questions, but no way to get answers. He was focused on his problem of getting home and was in no mood for foolishness.

Will saw Frank Sutton before he found Amanda. As usual, he was in one of his defensive moods and running his mouth.

"Guess you won't be bothering Amanda any more, huh. My father said Mayor James really let you have it last night. You should forget about her and find someone of your own status and leave the affluent alone."

Will stopped Blaze and stepped down from the saddle. He turned to Frank and slowly walked toward him.

"Why don't you repeat what you just said so I can make sure I heard you correctly." He grew more angry by the moment and hoped Frank would start something.

"Sure, I'll repeat it," he said as he looked around and saw people on the street beginning to pay attention to what was happening. "You are not fit to be with Amanda. You should be with those of your own status. If you have trouble understanding me, come over and I'll pound it into your thick head."

Frank was big, but he was soft and Will knew before he was done that he would inflict as much pain as possible without really hurting him. He stopped an arm length in front of Frank and said, "You were saying." He didn't get to finish before Frank threw a punch at him. Will ducked.

"You don't want to do this. You're going to get hurt."

Frank jabbed at him again, and Will dodge it by twisting at the waist to the left. At the same time Will unloaded a left hand to Frank's jaw and knocked him to the ground.

"I told you, boy. Don't mess with a man who knows he can kick your butt. You're not to smart if you do." Will paused and saw Abel Sutton standing in front of a clothing store. "I guess you aren't to smart though, huh. You have to have your daddy do your dirty work. You're not man enough to do it yourself," he said loud enough for all to hear. "Now get up and finish the fight you started or run with your tail between your legs."

Frank had let his anger get the best of him and was totally out of control. He charged Will like a raging bull and wanted him to pay for knocking him to the dirt.

"Better make this one good, boy. Your daddy's watching."

As Frank grabbed for Will, Will stepped to the side and hit Frank hard in the stomach and as he bent over and gasped for air he brought his knee up and kneed him in the face. Frank Sutton was out cold and lying in the middle of the street.

Will looked around the crowd for Frank's father.

"Mr. Sutton, it might be a good idea to get your son out of the street. He's liable to get run over."

"This isn't over Tidwell. I'm going for the sheriff."

"Oh no you don't, Abel. I been here from the start and your kid is at fault. You should be ashamed of the way your son talks to people." It was the Tucson county sheriff. He looked at Will and told him to get on about his business and then walked away. He too left Frank lying in the dirt.

Amanda was walking to work when Will found her. She smiled and said, "Good morning, handsome. Want to walk a girl to work."

"We need to talk. You know I really like you, don't you?'

"I was hoping so. Why."

"My fathers been shot and I have to leave for home early in the morning. I have to get home as quickly as possible."

"You're not going to ride Blaze are you? He's kind of old for a fast trip like you will be making."

"No. I got two tickets for the train from here to Las Cruces. I'll ride Blaze up the hill to home. He can make that part of the trip easy."

"Two tickets. You want me to....."

"No", Will interrupted. One for me and one for Blaze. I wish you could, but your father would never allow it. But I want you to wait for me. I'll be back for you."

"Yes, I'll wait for you. Just hurry and get back as soon as you can."

Amanda leaned forward and kissed him on the cheek. Will smiled, took her in his arms and gave her a real kiss, a kiss she wouldn't soon forget.

Chapter Twelve
Back Home Again

Will was up early and had Blaze, his saddle and his clothing ready to stow on the train when it arrived at the Tucson station. He waited impatiently in the station and drank a cup of coffee as he walked circles in the waiting room. The sun was just beginning to rise and already the sky was ablaze and exploding reds, yellows, and blacks shot across the horizon. It was going to be a beautiful morning, but Will would never know it. It was Amanda's arrival that stopped the circles and captured his attention and allowed him to taste the remainder of his coffee. She walked straight to him and gave him a tight hug and a passionate kiss. Their talk the night before changed her attitude toward Will and she didn't want him to leave.

As the train finally pulled into the station, Amanda took Will by the arm and walked with him to the platform. Will left her momentarily to make sure Blaze had feed and water and was secured properly. As he returned she said, "Hurry back, I'll miss you."

"I will," he said as he kissed her good-by and gave her a hug.

When the conductor called "all aboard", Will kissed her again and stepped on the train. Standing on the far end of the station platform he saw Frank Sutton and he had seen Amanda and him kiss before he boarded the train. He knew it would upset him and he hoped that Amanda would make it home without being confronted by the spurned aggressor. The train began to slowly pull away from the station and as it picked up speed Amanda grew smaller and smaller until she was gone. Will knew the trip to Las Cruces would be long without her so he tried to sleep. He had seen this part of the desert before and hadn't thought that much of it the first time so sleep seemed the right thing to do.

Each time the train stopped, Will went back to check on Blaze. He was handling the train ride well. He was eating and drinking plenty of water, so Will knew he would be okay. Will was so bored riding for such a long period on the train that he spent a couple of runs between stations in the stock car with Blaze.

When they finally pulled into the Las Cruces station, Will was happy the train ride was over. He found he liked standing on a motionless floor much more than on the constantly moving motion of the passenger car in which he had spent so much time the passed few days. Blaze came out of the stock car as he had gone in. The trip hadn't phased him at all. As he picked up his saddle and threw it on Blaze's back he saw her. He picked up his clothes and walked with Blaze to where Tessa Parker was standing on the station platform and she never took her eyes from him as he walked toward her.

"Didn't think I'd ever see you again," Tessa said as he approached.

"How's Mary and that broken arm of hers? Is she okay?"

"She healed up fine. It's my heart you broke. Do you always leave in the middle of the night or didn't you like me? I had a feeling you did. Have I made you feel bad enough or should I go on?"

As she talked, Will watched her every move and every curve of her body. She sure hadn't changed. She was as beautiful as ever and her dark brown hair shined in the late afternoon sun. Her green eyes sparkled as she talked and the black dress she wore looked to be made especially for her and was very flattering to her figure.

"Okay, I've had enough. What do I have to do to get you to forgive me?"

"Mary's train has been delayed and she won't be here until tomorrow, so you can buy me dinner for a start. Where are you headed now? I thought you were going to California."

"Made it as far as Tucson. Now I'm headed home. My fathers not doing to well."

"So you're headed back out our way again. I brought the surrey so you can ride part of the way in comfort and in shade. We'll be leaving early in the morning and at least you'll have someone to talk too. What do you say?"

"Sounds good to me. I like the company and as I remember Mary is quite the talker. I think I should learn a lot about you."

"You like the company, you say. That remains to be seen. I think you're afraid of me."

"Maybe so, but I guess I'll find out later. I've got to get a place for me and a stall for Blaze and I'd like to clean up before dinner."

"I have a room. You can clean up there if you'd like."

Will smiled and walked away toward the livery stable. Blaze, he thought, would be much easier to take care of than Tessa.

Twenty minutes later Will walked into the hotel closest to the train station to see about a room and found Tessa sitting in the lobby waiting for him. The Tucson Inn was a clean but older hotel. It was constructed of adobe and wood and the adobe was white washed and the wood painted green and white and everything was clean and dusted.

"This is the man I told you about," she said to the clerk as she walked to the registration counter. "He just came in on the train and he will be sharing my room."

The clerk looked at her, his face expressing surprise.

"Oh, don't have a heart attack," Tessa said. "We're married. We're here to pick up our daughter and her train won't be here until tomorrow morning." As they walked up the stairs to their room, she said "Do you think you can spend a whole night with me or will you leave again?"

Will was just getting dressed when Tessa walked back into the room with two cups of coffee. She smiled as she handed a cup to the man with whom she had spent the night.

"How are you this morning. You didn't seem to get much sleep last night."

"Great, I really feel great. How about you?"

She just kept smiling and drank her coffee.

Will looked through the window and said, "It's almost time to pick up Mary. I'll get Blaze and then the surrey. Are you hungry? I'm starving."

Mary had been to see her grandparents in Alabama and all the way to the Parker Ranch Tessa and Will heard about how green it was there and how the food there tasted different than the food here and how her mom had felt bad because she couldn't tell Bill good-by before he left and how she wished he had stayed with them. Do you think we should stop and let Blaze rest? He's no two year old you know. How's Bullet? Did he miss me?

Tessa told her daughter over and over to take a breath and let Will and her ears rest for a time. But Will was gaining valuable information and told her she could talk all she wanted. Mary was unknowingly embarrassing her mother and Will thought it was great. Tessa was even able to laugh as her daughter told stories on her. Will liked hearing her laugh and didn't mind it when she moved closer to him. Mary continued to tell Will whatever came into her mind and it came out that Tessa wasn't her real mother. The real one had died when Mary was born, but she loved her step mom for she had always treated her as her own.

Will found he didn't have to ask any questions to learn about Mary and Tessa. All he had to do was listen and Mary would tell him everything he wanted to know. Mary's constant conversation made the miles pass quickly and by mid afternoon they stopped the surrey in front of the house.

Maria, Tessa's cook and housekeeper, saw their approach and came out to meet them and Mary ran to her and gave her a big hug. Maria greeted Tessa and when she said "hello, Mr. Bill", Will was sure that he had been mentioned in conversation quite often. As Will gathered Mary and Tessa's bags to take them in the house, Maria said for him to leave them. She would get the help to carry the bags into the house. Will turned his attention to Blaze and walked him to the barn. Men working around the stable that was across from the bunkhouse watched him as he walked to the barn and wondered who this stranger could be.

Blaze was led to a freshly bedded stall and was given fresh hay and water. As the gelding ate, Will brushed his coat until the dust and dirt from the road was gone and his coat was again shiny. He would let him eat and rest before they started the last leg of their journey up the mountain to their home. He was so into caring for his horse that he hadn't seen Tessa enter the barn.

"In a big hurry to get up the hill?" she asked.

" I thought I was alone. You startled me."

"I can see that. Are you going to leave right away or in the morning? I think you should leave in the morning and let Blaze have a good rest before starting up the mountain. I've been up that way and it's no easy ride."

"I'm really worried about my dad and should leave now, but you are probably right. I should wait until morning."

"Good, it's settled then. I'll tell Maria you will be here for dinner. When you get done, come in the house and I'll get you a beer. Maria's made Mary's favorite, a roast , potatoes, carrots, with lots of gravy."

Will watched her as she walked to the house and he thought he had never watched Amanda James the way he watched and thought about Tessa. She was a beautiful woman and Amanda just a nice looking young woman with whom he liked to spend time. He didn't know what he would do about the two women, but knew he had to make a decision about them and he would have to make it soon. He knew Tessa was never far from his thoughts and he felt that she felt the same way.

When dinner was finished, Tessa, Mary and Will went out to the patio and Maria cleared the dishes from the table. The sun was down behind the hills to the west and the sky above them was ablaze in all the fiery colors. Tessa and Mary sat on a couch and Will in chair across from them. Mary talked and talked and Will listened to every word she spoke. Finally Tessa could take no more and interrupted her ramblings.

"Mary, it's been a long day and I think you should get some sleep if you want to be up in the morning to see Will off."

"It's early, mom. I don't want to go to bed yet."

"Come on, young lady. Let's get you to bed."

"Night Will. I will see you in the morning, won't I?"

"Yes, you'll see me. I won't leave until you do. Sleep well."

Darkness was upon them as mother and daughter disappeared into the house. Will got up to stretch and saw the lamp in Mary's room illuminate the curtains covering the window and then dim as she was tucked into bed.

When Tessa came out of the house she walked straight to him and took him by the arm. She held it tight and led him to the couch. As he put his arm around her he noticed a smiling face peeking through the window curtains. Mary was glad Will liked her mother.

Morning found Mary in the kitchen with Maria and Will tried to slip by and get to the barn before Mary saw him. As he walked out of the house he heard Mary call to him.

"Morning, Will. Maria and I are making you some breakfast"

The trail was long and in places steep as Will and Blaze made their way up the mountain to their home. He found himself thinking more about Tessa and Mary than the condition of his father and his family and this made him feel bad. But the farther he rode the more he missed the two he left down the mountain. He told them he would return as soon as he could, but he did have to help out around the ranch until his father was healed up enough to work himself. Two days later he rode through Lincoln and into the yard in front of his fathers home.

His mother was the first one out of the house followed closely by Grandma Rebecca and Grandpa Liam, but when his father walked out there came over him a truly heartfelt sense of relief. It was good to see him up and around and now he didn't feel so bad about the extra time he had spent with Tessa and Mary.

The hugs were many and the handshakes firm and honest and as it had always been done, the family ended up around the kitchen table and Will answered all their questions as best he could. It was when his mother, Bonnie, asked if he had met any nice girls while he was gone that the conversation got serious.

He told them of Amanda and of Tessa and Mary. As he told the family how he met Mary his mother got up and walked from the room. She returned to the kitchen with a telegram and handed it to him.

"What does it say, mom?" he asked.

"How should I know. It's addressed to you so I didn't read it."

Will opened the envelop and read the telegram and as he read a look of shock appeared on his face and it lost all its color. He folded the paper and put it back in the envelop and said nothing. Tears were welling in the corner of his eyes and he searched for her face in his mind, but it wasn't there. How could he have forgotten her so quickly?

"What is it Bill? Is it bad news?" his father asked.

"Yes, dad. She's dead. Amanda was shot and killed." He removed the telegram and read it aloud. It read, "Will. Amanda shot and killed by Frank Sutton. Found guilty and hanged. Mayor James.

"Who's Mayor James and who is this Will?" Bonnie asked.

He explained the situation in Tucson as best he could and how he somehow knew the Sutton family would come to no good. As for who Will was, he said, "Will is me." He thought it was going to take longer for him to explain why the name change came about than telling them of the sights and people he met along his way to Tucson and back.

"Enough talk about me. Who shot you, dad? Is he still alive? And what about the telegram you sent. It said dad was in a serious condition."

"No it didn't," his mother said. "The telegram I sent you said, 'Your father shot. Not serious. We're all okay. Miss you. Mom.' We really didn't expect you back so soon."

"Okay. It must have gotten messed up over the wire. Did you get the man that shot you, dad?"

"Yes, they're dead, but the man that sent them is still alive. His name is Maxwell Riley and he's from Louisiana. I can't believe he's carried a grudge for over twenty years."

"The New Orleans gambler, huh. He sent them, right."

"How did you know about that? I never told you that story."

"A good friend of yours I met in Las Cruces told me. Sometime when mom's not around I'll tell you what else he told me."

"Who did you talk to about me. I don't know anyone from Las Cruces."

"Sure you do. He was at your wedding. You only had two guests and he was one. It was Doc Franklin and the last thing he asked was if you still had General and the pinto that followed you around. He's a doctor in Las Cruces now and he said to tell you he still misses you and mom."

Grandma Rebecca got up from the table and walked across the kitchen and then walked back and handed Will a bowl full of cherry cobbler and a fork.

"Wait a minute. I've gotta get something." He walked outside and dug in the bottom of his saddlebags and then returned to the kitchen. "Here grandma. Don't say I don't listen to what you say." He handed her the fork she gave him the day he left home.

The routines of running the ranch were not forgotten, but the work load was doubled. Until his father could resume his job of running the ranch Will would have to stay and cover for him. There were two things that occupied his thinking and he planned for them both daily. One was Tessa and Mary and two was the man who for the third time had tried to kill his father. When his father was well enough to work he would use the excuse that he needed a break and go see Tessa and Mary. He would have Tessa cover for him while he went to Louisiana and got rid of the man who sought his fathers death. It wouldn't take that long if he took the train to and from New Orleans and if he could find the gambler. If he could find this man quickly the whole job would only take about a week.

"Good morning, son. I brought you a cup of coffee."

It was his mother that broke his train of thought.

"Thanks, mom. I can use it. I can see by the look on your face you want to know something. What is it?"

"I want to know about your friend Tessa. Tell me about her."

"There's not really much to tell. It's like I've known her all my life. She's my age, has dark brown hair, green eyes and is very nice to watch. What else can I say."

"If she has a daughter eight years old, how can she be your age. Something isn't adding up here and I want to know what it is."

"Mary is Tessa's stepdaughter. Her real mother died when Mary was born. Tessa loves Mary as if she were her own and Mary feels the same way about Tessa. They have a very special relationship."

"I'd like to meet this woman and her daughter. I can tell there's more to her than what you are telling me."

"I'm sure you will, mom. Thanks for the coffee. I've got to get back to work."

Six weeks after Will got home his father was ready to go back to work and run the ranch. The hills were covered with cattle and it was close to time to round them up and ship them off to market. Will knew if he was to pull off his plan to eliminate the threat to his father it had to be now, prior to roundup. He talked with his parents and they thought Josh, Will's father, could handle things so Will told them he was leaving to see Tessa. He would leave the following morning.

Blaze was able to keep up a blistering pace down the mountain and

Will was sitting on the patio in two days. After a happy reunion, Will told Tessa of his plan to go to Louisiana and how she would have to cover for him while he was gone. She agreed to help and would take him to Las Cruces and the train early in the morning and Blaze could stay at the ranch. As the sun set they decided to turn in early. With Mary tucked in and her lamp turned out, Tessa asked, "What's bothering you? It's not your trip, it's something else. What is it?"

"When I get back from Louisiana I want you to come with me to meet my parents, you and Mary."

"Are you sure that's what you want to do? We haven't know each other that long and I can't imagine what your mother would think about my showing up, especially with Mary."

"I'm sure, but if you don't want to, it's okay. I thought you felt like I do and you might want to make the trip with me. We can talk about it when I get back from New Orleans."

"Will, I...."

"We'll talk about it later, okay. Let's just be happy for the time we have now." He reached out and turned out the lamp.

Morning came quickly and everyone rushed around to get ready to make the trip to Las Cruces. Tessa wanted to talk to Will, but Mary kept her from saying what she wanted to tell him. Mary was her usual talkative self, but Will and Tessa said hardly a word. They made it to the train station with fifteen minutes to spare. Will gave Mary a hug and Tessa a kiss and started into the station. Just before he got to the door he turned and said, "I'm going to miss you two. Be careful going home and I'll see you in a week." He then walked into the station.

Tessa wrapped the reins around the surrey brake and jumped to the station platform. "He's not leaving like this," she said and rushed into the train station. She grabbed him and threw her arms around him and gave him a big kiss. "I love you too. And I will be here when you return."

Will pulled her to him and whispered in her ear, "I hoped you felt the same as me."

Mary stood in the doorway with a big smile on her face and as a woman tried to enter she said to her, "I'm getting a new daddy, ma'am. Isn't it wonderful."

Chapter Thirteen
New Orleans

As the New Orleans station came into view, Will could see the workers preparing to unload the goods transported to the city on the train. He had his valise in hand and was ready to start his search for the man who wanted his father dead. The train stopped and he stepped from the train to the platform and headed directly to the hotel closest to the station. He told Tessa he didn't remember the name, but he knew the hotel would be there and if necessary, she could reach him there.

The city had to be designed by an artist he decided and the artists palette was well used to come up with all the colors decorating the homes and businesses that lined the streets. The hotel in which he stayed was built of red brick and wood painted pure white while the store next door was built of wood and painted green. Next to it was one of yellow and then one of blue and another of grey. The city was the most colorful he'd ever seen.

He walked into the hotel, registered and then went directly to his room. He hung his clothes in the closet and as he removed them from the valise felt his old colt and pulled it out. The name Tidwell engraved in the handle of the colt he carried could get him in trouble here, he thought, and he pulled it from his holster and replaced it with the old one. He pulled the old colt from his holster and checked each chamber, twirled it and then replaced it in the holster. He practiced his draw several times and then walked from his room.

Finding a gambler in a city like New Orleans where gambling is a part of every hotel, saloon, and casino was going to be a time consuming job that required dedication and luck. He decided to start his search in the poker room of his hotel. It was a well furnished room with magnificent chandeliers and colorful drapes and ornate tables and chairs. Gambling was good here and the house cut kept the dealers paid, security in place and the room clean. The poker tables were full and as he walked through the maze of tables, Will watched and listened. He watched the faces of the players to learn those small things that allow a true professional to know if an opponent is bluffing or if he has a good hand. He listened hoping to hear the name Maxwell Riley a name that would end his search and set into motion his final plan. His search here ended, he moved on to the next gambling hall.

From poker palace to casino to hotel his search seemed to never end. It was late in the afternoon of his second day of searching that he met a gentleman at one of the bars he watched that pointed him in the right direction. Max Riley, he found, was making the rounds of the private games being held at various homes around the city. Now Will had to find a way to get himself invited to this exclusive mens club. He started by playing poker with the locals and found most of them were amateurs and easy prey for anyone that could read the deck and the faces of his opponents. As he played, he constantly talked of wanting to get into a big game where he could either make it big or go bust. A man standing against the wall Will felt was watching him. He was dressed well in a dark suit, white shirt with lace ruffles, a green and white tie and a black stovepipe hat. He seemed out of place in the hotel and looked as if he would be more at home in the big casino in the center of town. When a chair opened at the table where Will played, he asked if he might join the game.

"My name is Miles Tildon and I wonder if I might join your game, gentlemen. What, may I ask, is the buy in."

"Welcome to the game, sir. If you have money, we have the cards."

"And you are, sir? I didn't catch your name."

"Will Franklin. I'm just in from New Mexico and I'm looking for a big game. Whose turn is it to deal. Ante up. Let's play cards."

Mr. Tildon watched Will as he played each hand of poker, both his cards and his facial movements. After and hour or so, he got to his feet and tipped his chair to the table.

"Time for a short break. I'll be right back after I stretch. Mr. Franklin, would you care to join me?"

"Yes, sir. I could use a break and a drink from the bar."

"I understand you are looking for a big game, Mr.Franklin."

"Yes, I am."

"Let me do some checking and I may be able to help you. If you'll let me know where you are staying, I'll let you know what I find out. I should have an answer by eight o'clock tonight. Be ready for if there is a game, it will start at nine.

"Sounds good to me and I'll be ready at eight at my hotel. I'm staying at the St. James. I'll meet you in the lobby ."

The two men walked back to the table and Mr. Tildon excused himself from the game stating he had business to take care of and collected his money and left. Will sat back down at the table with a smile on his face. He was close to finding his prey and he would do it in someones private home with an affluent audience. For what more could he ask?

It was a hot and humid evening and the lobby of the St. James Hotel was crowded with people moving from the gaming room to the dinning room and it made Will nervous. He really didn't like crowds and preferred the open spaces of his home. He thought of Tessa to take his mind from the crowd and wished that she was with him. He laughed to himself and thought how he even missed Mary and her constant talking. It was the pungent odor of a woman's perfume that sent him outside the hotel and into the fresh air.

The sun was just about to set and a light breeze made the outside more bearable and the street began to come to life with people enjoying the gaiety of the city. The colors of the women's dresses and the men's suits attested to the ability of the dress makers and tailors to create a rainbow in motion moving on the street. The horse drawn carriages stopped only momentarily to allow parties to disembark and instantly were full again and headed for another part of the city. Night time seemed to bring New Orleans to life. And then Mr. Miles Tildon appeared in the crowd.

"Ah, Mr. Franklin. Enjoying the sights of the city?"

"Yes, sir, I am. I was just thinking the evening really brings this city to life."

"That it does, sir. We must be off, however, for their is a game you might like only a few blocks from here. Shall we go?"

"It's a game where money can be made?"

"Most certainly, sir. One of the better players in the city will be there tonight and he, as you stated earlier today, plays to make money or as you put it, go bust."

"Good. Let's be on our way."

"There is a one thousand dollar buy in and the game they play is five card stud. Can you manage the buy in?"

"Not a problem. Let's go play some poker."

The ride to the game took only minutes and the home was more a mansion than a house. Six large pillars were lined across the front and supported a large deck over the entrance. Carriages lined the drive and music could be heard from the inside. Ladies walked along the railing of the deck and watched the approach of their carriage.

The inside of the home was furnished lavishly and Will wondered if he had brought enough money to play in this game. The home owner was definitely a rich man. A butler answered the door and led them through the house to what Will thought was the library where five men stood talking around a mahogany lined poker table.

"Gentlemen, may I present Mr. Will Franklin of New Mexico. He is in the cattle business and has come to New Orleans to let off some steam and play some poker."

All five men wore suits and ruffled shirts and multicolored ties. As they introduced themselves, Will watched their faces carefully to see how their expressions showed when not under the pressure of playing for a large pot. Mr. McPherson, the owner of the home was the first to really speak.

"Gentlemen, shall we play poker. We can't play all night for our wives await our company."

The first few hands Will watched the other players and when he was satisfied he had their habits down, he began to play seriously. The next hand was the first hand Will really played and he bet small at first betting on the ace he held as a hole card. His first card up was a ten of spades and his second card up another ace. The betting was less than he expected so he bet one hundred dollars when his turn came. Two of the players dropped out and when his third card up was another ten, two more dropped out. Mr. McPherson and Will were all that were left and Will believed he was working on a straight. Will was holding two pair, tens and aces while McPherson showed a seven of hearts, an eight of spades, and a ten of clubs and he bet another one hundred dollars. Will watched his face and saw the telltale twitch at the corner of his mouth. He was bluffing. Will raised another one hundred dollars and McPherson called. The last card was dealt and without looking at it Will, having the pair of tens showing was first to bet. He looked at McPherson and bet another hundred dollars. McPherson looked at his hole cards, then at Will and back to his cards. He shook his head and threw his cards to the center of the table. The rest of the evening the cards were good to Will and when it was decided they had played long enough, Will was holding most of everyones money.

"Now that we are finished for the evening, I wonder if I might ask where someone as young as yourself learned to play cards so well?" Mr. McPherson asked.

"I've been playing poker since I was six years old with the ranch hands that work for my father. They taught me that there was more to poker than cards. They taught me to watch my opponents when they had good hands and when they have bad hands. It's not only the cards that beat you, it's how you handle them that let's people know if you have a good hand."

"I have a friend you might like to play poker with and he's quite good. His name is Maxwell Riley and I can find out where he will be playing next and get you an invitation if you'd like. The money you made here tonight will pay your buy in."

"I would really appreciate your help to get into a game like that. Thank you very much."

They shook hands and Will smiled for not only had he made good money from the game, he also got an invitation to play Riley. Things were going well and he hoped not too well.

Will now had the invitation he needed to get to Riley and it was time to formulate a plan that would set him up and make everyone think he was a cheat. If he were caught dealing from the bottom of the deck, palming cards, or using a marked deck, he would have him. How Riley reacted to being caught would determine how his game would end. Now he just had to wait for Miles Tildon to let him know where and when he would next play in a big game.

The morning came with lightning and loud claps of thunder and the rain came down in sheets. Will's plans to see the port were washed away and he decided to pass the day in his room and in the card parlor. Some card playing would keep him sharp and observant and ready to take on one of the best poker players on the gulf coast. He hoped his luck would last at least for one more big game. Staying around the hotel would also make it easy for Miles Tildon to find him.

As the rain continued throughout the day the memories of Tessa and home occupied his mind and he smiled as he remembered Mary telling him all about her mother. The more he remembered the more he wanted to be home with Tessa at his side. His parents and grand-parents were going to have one heck of a time keeping up with Mary and her constant chatter. They always said they wanted grandchildren and this one came ready made and eight years old.

Will went down to the registration desk to check for messages left for him and when there were none went to play poker. The tables weren't full as they had been the previous day, but he managed to get a seat at the one with the most action. Within an hour there were only two left at the table and Will was about to take the last of his money. The last hand they played his opponent had an ace and two kings showing. Will's consisted of an ace, king and ten of hearts. The bet to Will was fifty dollars. Will saw his fifty and raised another fifty. Before the last card was dealt, his opponent called.

"I have you beat with the cards I have showing," his opponent said as he looked at his last card. "My hand is even better now."

"That may be true, but we'll know for sure in a minute. You have the pair of tens so bet." Will looked at his last card and smiled.

"I bet another fifty dollars," his opponent said with a big smile on his face. He knew he had this hand won.

"I'll see your fifty and raise another fifty."

"You must really like to throw your money away, sir. Your fifty and one hundred more. Now will you let me win?"

"No, sir. I still have money left. I'll see your one hundred and raise fifty more. How proud of your cards are you now?"

"I'll see your fifty and call. Let's see if you can beat a full house, kings over aces."

"This just isn't your day, friend. I've got you beat." He slowly lined his last card up with the others and it was a jack of hearts. "I'm one card away from a royal flush. Think I've got it?" He picked up his hole card and dropped it in the center of the table. It was a queen of hearts and completed his royal flush.

"I don't believe it. No one has that kind of luck." He got up from the table and was still complaining as he walked out of the card parlor.

"Sometimes it doesn't pay to play cards, and it is a wise man that quits before he loses it all."

Miles Tildon smiled as Will spoke. He saw the man beat by the royal flush and he thought Will was one of the luckiest poker players he had seen, but that would be determined at another time and at a much larger game.

"I have good news for you, my friend. The big game you seek will take place tomorrow night at eight o'clock. I will pick you up and deliver you to the game."

"That sounds good, Mr. Tildon." Will extended his hand to shake hands and passed Tildon a one hundred dollar bill for his help. "Don't take it wrong, friend. I really appreciate your help."

"Not at all, Mr. Franklin. And thank you very much. It is my job, you know, to search out poker players worthy of my benefactors time and talents."

"So you work for Max Riley?"

"Oh, no sir. I work for the gentleman that will host tomorrows game, Mr. Reginald Bookins. He's one of the richest men on the gulf coast. Have you heard of him?"

"I believe so. Doesn't he own a fleet of cargo ships. I think he owns a riverboat too, the River Queen I believe."

"You are well informed, Mr. Franklin. He does own those things and many others. Nothing moves on the gulf coast that Mr. Bookins doesn't have his hand in."

"I couldn't keep up with all of the businesses he owns. I wouldn't even want to try. I have trouble enough running a cattle ranch and making the books come out right."

"I must be off now and I will be here to escort you to the game tomorrow at seven o'clock. Be ready, Mr. Franklin. Tomorrow you will have much more than the game you seek. To make it fair for all players, there will be a buy in of five thousand dollars and once it's gone, your game is over."

"Until tomorrow, Mr. Tildon."

"Until tomorrow, Mr. Franklin."

Time was beginning to run short. The poker game would be played tomorrow, Sunday, and he had to catch a train home on Monday. It didn't leave much time for a change of plans if play required it or for unseen problems that might arise. But he was in it now and no matter what he would have to make do with whatever was at hand.

The day of the big game was just the opposite of what Will had expected. Instead of the hours dragging by, they seemed to fly and before he knew it, it was time to dress and go down and meet Miles Tildon. He was nervous, but not about the game. It was not knowing how Max Riley would react to being called a cheat that bothered him. That and the fact he would be playing in Riley's home surroundings and he didn't know which of the people watching the game were there to protect him. He had to catch him making a mistake he couldn't walk away from or allow his bodyguards to enter into the proceedings. He knew he had to play as he had never played before and watch his opponents every move to bring his plan to his desired outcome.

The lobby of the St. James was unusually quiet for a Sunday evening and as he waited for his escort to the game walked into the poker parlor and watched the tables. There were quite a few men playing at the tables and Will now knew that New Orleans was truly a city of gamblers.

"Mr. Franklin, good evening." It was Miles Tildon.

"Good evening, sir. Are we off to the game?"

"Yes, sir. But the location of the game has changed. We won't be the guests of Mr. Bookins as the game now will be played at the casino. Nothing has changed other than the location of the game."

"Do any of the players have any connection to the casino?"

"Mr. Riley is a part owner of the establishment. Why do you ask?"

"I like to know who and what I am up against when I play poker."

"What do you mean by that, Mr. Franklin? I assure you the game will be played by those at the table and there will be no interference from the gallery. Should there be, I assure you that I myself will have your back." He opened his coat and showed Will the two pistols he had in his waistband.

"I knew you were carrying. I noticed them the first time I met you. It is good, however, to know that I can count on someone other than myself should a problem arise."

"I am at your service, sir. You may feel at ease as I will keep a sharp eye on the table and the gallery."

The casino was a grand structure with an entry protruding out into the lavish landscaping of manicured grass and multicolored flower beds shaded by immense weeping willow trees. The inside of the entry was decorated with paintings and statuary depicting those who had owned and cared for the gambling establishment over the years. The casino floor was covered with poker tables, pharaoh tables, and long bars with brass trim and footrests. The gamblers were a myriad of cultures and as colorful in their dress as the flower beds that graced the casino entry.

There were three women Will could see on the casino floor that were gambling and he hoped he wouldn't be playing with them at his table. Normally women were not allowed on the casino floor and this lead him to believe that they were professional gamblers. Miles Tildon led him to a table where three men waited and as they approached the table the men stood.

"Gentlemen, may I introduce Will Franklin. He is a cattleman from New Mexico and has expressed a desire to play poker with you gentlemen. Mr. Franklin, this is Mr. Bookins, Mr. Jamison, and Mr. Riley. Enjoy your game, gentlemen. This should prove to be an interesting evening. Mr. Franklin is quite adept at poker playing."

The four men shook hands and exchanged greetings and then sat down at the table. Mr. Bookins related the rules by which they would be playing. It was to be dealers choice as to what game would be played and there would be no extra buy ins. Once you lost your original buy in, you were done for the night. No weapons of any kind would be allowed at the table, so if you will open you coats so we may insure there are none it would be appreciated. All four men accommodated him and then he continued.

"Are these rules as conveyed appropriate and what you had expected, Mr. Franklin? I do hope we can have an enjoyable evening."

"Are there any rules to cover a players sitting out a hand?"

"No, Mr. Franklin. Should you desire to do so, that is your right. I would hope, however, that such an occurrence wouldn't happen too often."

"I like to play poker, gentlemen. I believe five card stud is the only game that really let's one know if a person is a poker player or just someone sitting at the table."

"Do you like to play high hand or low hand when you play?"

"Either is fine as long as it is not a high low split. If I am going to work for a pot, I surely don't want to split it with someone else. Guess I'm sort of selfish in my way of thinking."

"No, sir. It is your right to feel as you do. However, others at the table may not feel as you do."

"That is their right, sir, and in such a situation I would choose to sit the hand out. I don't want to seem unfriendly, but it's the way I learned to play. Those that taught me said there were many ways to play poker, but most were thought up by those who are really just amateurs."

"Gentlemen, Max Riley interrupted, let's play poker. I think Mr. Franklin has made his point as have we. A new deck of cards, please. If there are no objections, I will deal first." He broke the seal on the box and removed the cards and began to shuffle. It was apparent that his hands were soft and accustomed to the feel of a deck of cards.

The first few hands went slowly as each player watched the manner of Will's play looking for any sign that might give away whether he held a good or bad hand. They could find none. At the same time, Will watched his opponents and found Mr. Jamison to be the least proficient at poker. He smiled when he had a good hand and frowned when he had a bad one. Mr. Bookins was a much better poker player and it took a while for Will to learn his habits. He found if he held a good hand, he had a tendency to tap his fingers on the table and if it were bad, the right side of his mouth twitched.

Max Riley was a true professional. Will could find nothing that gave away the hand he held. As the time passed, Mr. Jamison lost his five thousand dollar buy in and left the table. It was evident he was upset at the loss of his money and asked how they knew what he held in his hand.

"It isn't that we knew what you had in your hand, we just knew if it was good or bad," Will said. "If you held a good hand you showed a slight smile and if it was anything less, the corners of your mouth turned down. Poker is more than a game of cards. It is knowing the habits of your opponents and learning to interpret them. Thank you for playing, Mr. Jamison. I really enjoyed your participation in the game."

As Jamison walked away, Mr. Bookins asked, "What have you found in me that gives away my hand?"

Mr. Bookins, you're still a player. You don't really think I would give away that kind of information now, do you? I think we should play cards and talk later."

"Here, here," Riley said. Let's get back to cards."

Max Riley and Will were staying just about even and Bookins was on his way out. He lasted four more hands and then was out.

"If you don't mind, gentlemen, I would like to remain and watch the rest of your game."

"It's okay with me," Will said. "I like the company. How about you, Mr. Riley. Is it okay with you?"

"It's fine with me. Can we please get back to the game? These constant interruptions break my train of thought."

"Is that all it takes to disrupt your game? I guess I'm just accustomed to playing with cowboys and interruptions don't bother me."

"Well, we're not in your New Mexico and I suggest we get back to play. It's your deal, so deal."

"Just one more thing if you don't mind, Mr. Riley. Mr. Bookins, you asked earlier how I knew the hand you held, right."

"Yes, Mr. Franklin."

"If you hold a good hand, you tap the fingers of your right hand on the table. If you hold a bad one, the right side of your mouth twitches. These are habits that Mr. Riley has probably known for years." Will tried to keep the conversation going for he knew now it irritated Mr. Riley.

"If you don't mind, let's get back to the game or retire to the bar and keep up the conversation. At this point I don't care which we decide to do."

"Easy, Mr. Riley. I'm ready to continue. How about you?"

Will had Riley on edge and tried to keep him there. If he could, he was more apt to make a mistake. As they played he kept talking and asking Riley questions attempting to break his train of thought again. It took about another two hours, but it finally happened, he got to Mr. Riley.

"I grow tired of your constant questions and idle chatter, so I suggest we play one last hand to decide who will be the winner here tonight."

"Two final questions if you don't mind."

"All right. Two more questions and then we finish the game."

"Do you have a family, Mr. Riley?"

"No. My business keeps me on the road and I've never had time for a family."

"Have you any brothers or sisters?"

"No, I haven't. I had two brothers but they were killed some years ago."

"Thank you, Mr. Riley. I like to know about the people I'm about to take down. Shall we play poker?"

The last hand played was five card stud and Max Riley was the dealer. The first card dealt down to Will was and ace of spades and the first card up a king of diamonds. Riley's first card up was an ace of clubs and Riley bet one hundred dollars and Will called. The second card up to Will was a king of hearts giving him a pair of kings. The last hand of their night brought all who remained in the casino to their table and they watched in silence. As Will looked at the crowd he saw Miles Tildon and he nodded in acknowledgement. The second card up to Riley was a deuce of clubs, a possible flush. Will bet five hundred dollars and Riley called. Both men held hands that were possible winners, but there were two cards to go and they would determine the winner. The third card dealt to Will was an ace of diamonds. With his hole card he held two pair, aces and kings and he felt he had a good chance of winning. Riley's third card up was an ace of hearts and the aces were gone. Riley's two aces were the high hand so it was his bet. He pushed one thousand dollars into the pot and sat back and smiled. Will called. The last card dealt came face up and it would decide who would be the winner.

Will had not been able to find any habit in Riley's game that might let him know what kind of hand he was up against. He knew he would never again play a game of poker such as had been played this night and he had enjoyed it thoroughly. It was too bad it had been played for the reason Will had wanted, to flush out Riley. He couldn't think of anything to do to get him branded as a cheat for his game was flawless. If it came down to it, win or loose, he would have to call him out. Will looked at the card just dealt him and it was a queen of hearts and he ended up with two pair, aces and kings. Riley's last card was a deuce of hearts and his two pair was still the high hand and it was his turn to bet.

"Let's make this last pot one worth having," Max Riley said. "Twenty thousand dollars is a lot of money and I suggest either you or

I walk out with all of it. Does that sound good to you? We have been just about even with our winnings all evening, so I suggest for this last pot we go all in." He pushed all the money in front of him into the pot.

"I agree," Will said and placed all of his money in the pot. "I call."

Will having called Riley's hand required his opponent to show his hand first and as he turned his hole card over Will knew he had him. He didn't have to prove Riley a cheat, he had done it to himself. The card he turned over was an ace of spades.

"We have a real problem here," Will said. "It seems the deck we're using has five aces in it and two of them are aces of spades." He turned over his hole cards showing the ace of spades and watched Riley's face. "It seems I win and you, sir, are a cheat. As you were dealer, I wonder where you found that extra ace of spades."

Maxwell Riley jumped to his feet and pulled a derringer from beneath his vest and aimed it at Will and cocked the hammer. It was then that a shot was heard from behind him and Maxwell Riley fell to the floor.

"Thank you, Mr. Tildon. Your shot was well placed. Right in the heart.

You are a true and capable friend and I applaud the attention you paid to the game. Knowing now what you told me regarding my poker playing habits, Mr. Franklin, I can't imagine the amount of money he has stolen from me. I thank you." Mr. Bookins extended his hand to Will.

Will walked to where Miles Tildon was standing and they shook hands as he said, "Thank you for saving my life. I really don't know how to thank you."

"Nonsense, my friend. I told you I would back you if trouble arose and was glad to be of assistance. I never did like the man for he had a habit of looking down on people not as fortunate as himself. Unlike you, few people liked him. I might suggest you gather up your winnings before someone else helps you."

"Mr. Bookins, Miles, if you would care to join me at the bar, the drinks are on me, at least until the police show up.

"Police?" Mr. Bookins asked. "Why would the police be called to such an establishment as this? Can you see anything that might be of interest to them? Look around. Is anything different from when you came in?"

Will looked around and the crowd that circled their table was gone or playing poker and the body of Maxwell Riley was gone. As they drank at the bar, Will decided to tell them the truth and when he had finished Miles laughed.

"Years ago Riley tried to get me to go after a man named Joshua Tidwell, your father I gather. Knowing you now makes me happy I decided not to accept his contract."

"Me too. And always remember, if you are ever in Lincoln, New Mexico you are both always welcome in my home."

It was near four o'clock in the morning when Will made it back to his room in the St. James Hotel and he had to be at the station to catch his train by six. He quickly packed his clothes and strapped on his gun and checked out of the hotel. When he got to the train station he told the clerk he would be asleep in the waiting room and to wake him for the train west.

"Yes, sir, Mr. Tidwell. I heard what you did tonight. I'll wake you in plenty of time for the train. And before you ask, nothin' goes on in this town I don't know about." He opened his vest and Will saw the star on his chest that read deputy sheriff.

Chapter Fourteen
Tessa Parker's Ranch

Tessa was on the Las Cruces station platform just as she had promised she would be when Will left and as he stepped from the train she walked to meet him. Her white dress, red scarf and dark brown hair moved gently with the evening breeze that blew across the platform from the west.

Her green eyes never left him and the closer she got, the more they sparkled. Will took her in his arms and hugged and kissed her and told her how much he had missed her. He held her tight as they walked and when he asked where the surrey was, she said it was at the livery stable.

"I thought we could use a little time to ourselves before going back to the ranch so I have a room at the hotel just down from the livery where we will spend the night before going home tomorrow. Is that okay with you?"

"You know it is. I guess you know where you want to eat supper too. I'm hungry."

"Of course. I have it all planned right down to where I take you back to the room where we can be alone."

"That all sounds good, so let's go eat so we can get on with the evening."

As they ate their supper they talked of Will's trip and how Max Riley had been killed. They talked of the money he had made at the poker tables and how much he had missed her. He told her how he missed the feel of her body next to him in the middle of the night and how he wanted to feel her there again. It was then that a man approached their table.

"Good evening, Tessa. I don't think I've met your friend."

"Walter Ramsey this is Will Tidwell, a friend of mine from Lincoln."

"Nice to meet you, Will. You related to Liam Tidwell? He shot me when I was a young man. Best thing that ever happened to me. Caused me to grow up and start a business of my own and I've been busy every since."

"Nice to meet you, sir. What business are you in?"

"Cattle. Been tryin' to get Tessa here to sell me her place ever since her husband died, but she won't sell. Stubborn little gal, isn't she."

"She runs a tight ranch and doesn't seem to have many problems. She's probably doing what she wants and you can't blame her for that."

"That may be true, son, but I'll keep tryin'. She's got some really nice grassland I sure could use. I got a lot of cattle and grass is what I need and it's sparse this year. You know, no rain. Tessa here has plenty for her herd and if she'd sell, I'd run some of my cattle in there with hers."

"Good luck, sir. I think you have a real job trying to get her to sell. Been nice meeting you."

"Think you'll ever sell Tessa?"

"I don't know yet, Walter. Time will tell. Have a nice evening."

"You two enjoy yourselves and I'll see you later."

As Walter walked away Will noticed he had a limp. Grandpa must have shot him in the left leg when he was young, he thought.

"Are you about ready to leave?" Will asked of Tessa.

"I thought you'd never ask. Remember what you said on the station platform? You said you liked lying close to me. Well, I feel the same way, so let's go to the room."

"One question before we leave."

"Okay."

"How did you get away without Mary throwing a fit?"

Tessa just smiled and they left.

Will was up early the following morning and went to the livery stable and picked up the surrey and then started back to the hotel for Tessa. He stopped at a cafe and picked up two cups of coffee and a couple of sweet rolls and talked to the minister from the church next door. When he entered their room Tessa was still in bed and he sat the coffee and sweet rolls on the table and walked over to her. He ran his hand under the covers and she woke up.

"Coffee's ready and I have a sweet roll for you. Think you might make it out of bed today?"

"I don't know. I haven't recovered from last night yet. Will you hand me some coffee, please."

"Nope. You've got to get up and get dressed and wear a dress. I have a surprise for you."

"I don't have a clean one with me. I'll have to wear the white one I wore yesterday."

"White. That's fine," he said with a smile. "You will look just as beautiful as ever. Come on, get busy. I'm in a hurry. I'll take our bags down and load them in the surrey."

Tessa dressed, washed her hands and face and brushed her hair and had no idea why Will was in such a hurry. She drank her coffee and ate her sweet roll as she walked down the stairs to where Will was waiting. He took her coffee cup and set it in the back of the surrey and then took her by the hand and lead her to the church just up the street from the hotel. He stopped as they neared the door.

"Tessa Parker, do you love me?"

"Yes, I do."

"Enough to marry me?"

"Yes, and I will."

He reached into his right pants pocket and pulled out an engagement ring and slipped it on her finger.

Will opened the door and lead Tessa up the aisle to where the minister waited. Ten minutes later they were Mr. and Mrs. William Tidwell and he took the ring from his left pocket and placed it on her finger. He had guessed correctly. The young woman in the New Orleans jewelry store was the same size as Tessa.

The ride to the Parker Ranch was spent talking of how their lives would now change and how much better it would be for all concerned. It was Mary that had Will bothered. How would they tell her she had a new dad without first asking how she felt about him marrying her mother. Tessa told him he was worrying for nothing for he was a hero in her eyes. He had saved her life.

Mary ran out of the house as Will and her mother rode up to the front of the house and gave them both a big hug. She immediately started with the questions of how their trip had gone and she was ready to relate all that had happened around the ranch while her mother was gone. It was Maria who noticed the rings on Tessa's finger and she congratulated them and said it was a good reason for there to be a big fiesta. As Tessa and Mary walked to the house, Maria waited for Will.

"Mr. Bill, I mean Mr. Will, you make Tessa a very happy woman. Mary will be happy too when you tell her you her new father. You make me happy too. If Tessa and Mary are happy, I am happy."

"Thank you, Maria. I appreciate the way you take care of them."

"Come, Mr. Will. I will get you something to eat. You must be hungry."

As they started toward the house, Mary burst through the door and threw her arms around Will and said, "I love you, dad. I'm glad you're here with me and mom. I hoped you would be my new dad when you found Bullet and me in the desert. I knew you'd be a good one."

After supper Tessa, Mary and Will went out on the patio where a soft, cooling breeze blew in from the west. As they talked Tessa told

Will about the ranch of which he was now part owner and of the cattle that grazed two miles northwest of the ranch house. She also told him of the foreman and his family that lived in the house not far from the bunkhouse where the seven men who worked for her lived. Maria, she explained, had her own room in the house and was considered part of the family.

"You didn't realize what you were getting yourself into when you married me, did you?" Tessa said as she smiled and reached out for his hand.

"It isn't any different than what I grew up with," he said as he took her hand and sat down beside her. "I've lived on a ranch and worked cattle my whole life and the older I get the more I like it."

"Tomorrow we'll ride out and I'll show you everything I've told you about. It will surprise you for you can't describe the colors of the desert with words. I'll introduce you to the men I've told you about and let them know you are now their new boss."

"Sounds good to me," he said and smiled at the thought of her wondering if he could run her ranch. The Parker Ranch encompassed a little more than ten thousand acres. His family ranch covered more than three hundred thousand acres and his mothers parents ranch over one hundred thousand acres. He was sure he could manage Tessa's ranch. "If you have a good and honest foreman it makes the job much easier."

"It's getting late and if we're to see the ranch tomorrow, we'll need an early start. Mary, time for bed. Off with you and I'll be in shortly to tuck you in."

"That sounds like a good idea, We have a marriage to consummate this night, you know."

"Mom, what does consummate mean?"

"Ask your new father. He has to learn quickly that there are some things that are better said in private."

"Will, what does it mean. And can I call you dad?"

"I wish you would. Consummate means to make something complete or perfect. In this case it means that your mother is the perfect woman for me. Do you understand now?"

"Yes, dad," Mary answered. "Good night, dad. You could come in a tell me good night if you want too."

"Thank you, Mary. I'll be in shortly. Now off with you and get to bed."

When Mary left the room Tessa said, "You got yourself out of that one, but there will be many more times we'll have to watch what we say when Mary is around. She doesn't miss much and you can never be sure what she will say or do when others are around. It could prove embarrassing. Now then, you were saying something about consummation."

They both went in and wished Mary good night and then walked to their room arm in arm.

The sun was rising and the cottonwood trees around the house cast long morning shadows across the square between the house and barn. The breeze that cooled last evening was gone and the dry desert air was warming as the beams of sunshine lighted the day. Men were leaving the field kitchen and heading out to start their days work and the women cleared the dishes from the table and prepared for a days work in the gardens that furnished fresh vegetables and potatoes.

Will walked to the barn and found Blaze already eating his hay and oats as was Bullet and the other horses. While waiting for the horses to finish, he looked around the barn and found an old map rolled up and stuck on the back of a seldom used work bench. On the map was plotted where water was to be found just below the surface of the ground and all within the borders of the ranch. In all, there were twelve separate locations and spaced in such a manner that made irrigation of the dry acreage possible. Wells could be dug to furnish water for the cattle and would increase the amount of grazing area. He couldn't understand why no one had put the map to use sooner. He rolled it up and stuck it in his shirt and as they rode the ranch he would see where these wells and windmills would have to be built.

The day was half gone when they were approached by a man riding a pinto and coming from the direction where Tessa's cattle grazed. He wore a Mexican sombrero and carried a Winchester rifle in his hand.

"Will Tidwell, this is Ray Browning my ranch foreman."

"Nice to meet you Mr. Browning.

"Hi, Ray. What you doing over here. The cattle and…

"Mary, mind your manners. Mr. Browning does and goes where he thinks it is necessary."

"That's all right Mrs. Parker. She means well."

"It's Mrs. Tidwell now, Ray. Will and I were married in Las Cruces yesterday."

"Yes, ma'am. I didn't know. I guess I'll be getting my orders from you now, Mr. Tidwell. What can I expect in the way of changes?"

"Not much. Just keep doing your job and I'll be happy. I'm looking for ways to expand our grazing area and more water. We can always use more water."

As they continued his first look at the ranch, Will watched for any sign of survey or possible well locations that might have been left by the maker of the map he found. Though he found none, he was sure he could find the water locations and install pumps to bring the water to the surface. But he would worry about the wells and water when he returned to the ranch after visiting his parents in Lincoln.

When the sun began to drop behind the mountains in the west the evening breeze began to blow and the three dismounted their horses and walked them into the barn. A young Mexican boy took them and Tessa, Mary and Will walked to the house. Will said they would have to go up the mountain soon to allow his family to meet his new wife and daughter. They would leave early in the morning the day after tomorrow.

The following day Will talked to the cowhands that had been with the Parker Ranch the longest to see if any were around when the survey for water was made. Several, he found, were around but had nothing to do with the survey or knew why it was conducted. Mr. Parker had a plan, but had not discussed it with anyone who worked on the ranch. Will went out again to try and figurer out what it was that the map would ultimately achieve. Mary, who had accompanied him was the one to help solve the mystery of the map.

"Did you find that old drawing in the barn, dad? Dad, are you listening to me?"

"I was thinking, Mary. What was it you said?"

"Did you find that old drawing in the barn?"

"Yes, why do you ask?"

"I know where there is another one like it and another one is in the house."

"Will you show me where they are?"

"Sure. Let's go back and I'll show you."

The ride back to the house was quite enlightening for Mary's father had told his daughter of his plan to improve the ranch. It was clear, though, that the time that had passed since her fathers death left holes in the story she related. When they got back to the barn, Mary went to a corner of the barn where she had hidden away things that brought back memories of her father. She pulled out another rolled up drawing and handed it to Will.

"Is this what you are looking for, dad? I keep it to remind me of my real dad. Is that okay?"

"Of course it is, Mary. You don't ever want to forget your father. He will always be special to you as he should be. But you remember, I'll always love you too."

Mary smiled as Will opened the rolled up drawing. It was a simple drawing of what looked like ditches that ran from well site to well site and ended in a reservoir that collected the excess water.

"Mary, was your father going to grow hay here on the ranch?"

"He said he wanted to grow something, but I can't remember what it was."

"That's okay. Will you show me the picture in the house that shows what your father had in mind?"

"Sure, come on. It's on the wall in the hall that goes to my bedroom. I'll show you. Let's go."

The picture was right there in front of him and he hadn't know its true meaning. It was a birds eye view of the well sites, the ditches connecting them, the reservoir and a large green area Will thought to be a hay field. If this dream of Mary's father was constructed, it would double or triple the number of cattle that could be raised on the ranch. It looked to Will that the wells would irrigate about one thousand acres of hay and furnish water for the livestock. It would also make the ranch worth ten times what it would bring now. Will wondered if Tessa was aware of what her husband had in mind and decided to find out.

Tessa was in the ranch office updating the books for it was near payday for her help. She sat with her back to a window and the sun shining in caused her hair to look more red than dark brown. As Will and Mary walked into the room she looked up and smiled.

"Okay, what have you two been up to this morning? Have you seen anything you'd like to change as you've been looking around?"

"No I haven't. You seem to have everything well in hand. But I do have a question for you. Were you aware of any plans your husband had for improving the ranch?"

"Will, you are my husband. Mary's fathers name was Russell and everyone called him Russ. As for improvements, he always wanted to be able to raise more cattle, but I don't recall any major changes he wanted to make."

"I think he was about to make some big changes and if he hadn't been killed, they would probably be done already. He talked to Mary about it and she is the one who put the puzzle I found together. She's a smart little lady. When we come down off the mountain, I think I'll look into this a little deeper, that is if Mary will help me. What do you say, Mary?"

"Sure I can. You just say when you want to go," Mary answered.

Chapter Fifteen
In-Laws and OutLaws

It was good to see the pines again and smell their scent that was carried on the wind blowing in from the south. The sagebrush and cactus of desert floor was far behind and Will felt as if he were back in God's country. Tessa drove the surrey and Will and Mary rode Blaze and Bullet.

Had Tessa not needed to bring half of her closet, they wouldn't have needed the surrey and they would have been much farther up the mountain. But if it made her happy, then all was well. Mary rode into the trees from side to side of the trail and was having the time of her life. She had never seen such trees in person and couldn't believe their size or their number.

"How much farther is it to your ranch, dad?"

"You're there. We've been on Tidwell land for the passed three hours. It's probably about four or five more miles to the house."

"How much land do you own?"

"Almost enough. Any more would make it really hard to keep an eye on."

"Where's all your cattle?"

"They're higher up the mountain in the high meadows this time of year. As we get closer to the house you'll see a few head, but most are up in the high meadows eating good mountain grass and getting fat."

Will thought Mary's questions would never end and was glad his parents would soon be the targets of her conversation. It was evident that Tessa knew she had found the right man for Mary's own father would have told her to be quiet hours ago.

R. J. STEPP

"Mary, be quiet and listen to the trees talk to you. The wind makes the trees talk to each other. Don't you wish you knew what they said to each other? Let's be quiet for a spell and listen to them talk, okay."

"Okay, mom. I'll be quiet. But I know trees don't talk, but I'll listen."

Will watched Tessa as she spoke to her daughter and thought how fortunate he was to have her for his wife. She was everything he wanted in a woman. She was beautiful, a wonderful companion, a good mother and smart. She was a business woman the likes of which he had never seen before, but could also be the most tender hearted and caring person he had ever met. He rode Blaze to the side of the surrey and stepped on the back and tied his horse to the back of the wagon. As he climbed to the front, Tessa moved over and handed him the reins.

"I was hoping you would ride with me for a while," Tessa said and moved closer to him. "I like having you close."

"It's not too much farther now and I don't want any of the hands working around the house to think you might be available," he said with a laugh. "You're mine and it's going to stay that way."

Half an hour later as the sun began to drop below the tops of the pines, the lighted windows of the main house came into view. The house was snuggled into the trees and they shadowed the big home. A few more minutes and they would reach his parents home and his family.

Bonnie, Will's mother, was the first one out of the house followed closely by Rebecca, Liam and Josh, Will's father. Within minutes Tessa and Mary knew that they were a welcome part of the family. Mary wasn't herself, though, for she hadn't said a word. Grandma Rebecca put her arm around Mary and said, "I bet you're hungry and tired after your long ride, sweetie. You come with me and I'll get you some peach cobbler. That'll make you feel better."

Bonnie said they should all go inside and as usual, they all gathered around the kitchen table where Tessa and Will spent the rest of the evening answering questions about how they met and where she lived and all about Mary. Before the evening ended, Tessa knew everything there was to know about Will, and the family knew all there was to know about Tessa and Mary.

Will got his father away from the others long enough to let him know he would no longer have to worry about Maxwell Riley. He was rather proud of the fact he had taken a professional gambler at his own game and that his cheating had gotten him killed all in the same evening. And he hadn't had to do the shooting.

"When you left in such a hurry to see Tessa, I thought there was more to it than that. I would have stopped you if I had known," Josh said. "Thank you for what you did, but please don't try it again. You could have been killed yourself. Let's just keep this between us, okay. Your mom doesn't need to know. We better get back to the others before they know we're gone."

As Will and his father rejoined the family in the kitchen, everyone had decided they were happy to have Tessa and Mary as part of the family.

As part of that family, there were chores that needed to be done and stock to be fed early in the morning. It was Bonnie's way of saying it's time for bed. Will and Tessa could have Will's old room and Mary would have the spare bedroom at the end of the hall. With all the good nights said, Tessa and Will tucked Mary in and then walked to Will's room.

"Remember what you said about my not knowing what I married into when I married you," Will said to Tessa. "I think we're even now, wouldn't you say?"

"I was holding nothing back compared to you. You never said anything about being so well off. I can't believe you kept all of this back. And your parents and grandparents, I already feel I've know them forever. They're nothing like what I expected."

"You think so, huh. Just wait, you'll see the other side before long."

When they were in the bedroom and the door was closed, Will sat on the edge of the bed and said, "Come here beautiful. I want to snuggle."

Will thought he was up early and went out to the kitchen for a drink of water and found Rebecca and Bonnie busy preparing breakfast. He gave them both a hug and then started down the hall to get Tessa and Mary.

"If you're looking for your daughter, she got up with grandpa and they're in the barn or the garden. She's really a worker. I saw her hauling hay for the horses," Bonnie said.

"She's already got your grandfather wrapped around her little finger," Grandma Rebecca said. "She's a talker and he likes that. I think he likes having a little girl around because she'll listen to him. She'll keep him occupied all day and it will be good for him. He needs to be needed and Mary will be just what he wants, someone he can answer questions for."

"It'll keep him young."

"If he can put up with her it might help keep him young, mom, but she can talk your ear off."

"I didn't notice that last night. She was so quiet you wouldn't know she was around."

"Believe me, she knows you today. Your turn is coming and don't say I didn't warn you."

Tessa's entering the room changed the subject and she apologized for being up so late. "Where's Mary? She's not bothering anyone, is she? What can I do to help?"

"Have a cup of coffee and join in the conversation. We've got everything under control and we've been talking about Mary. Grandpa Liam has been needing someone like Mary to keep him on his toes and make him feel needed. He's not as young as he used to be and Mary will keep him active," Grandma Rebecca said.

"I better get busy or dad will be calling me a slacker. You three Mrs. Tidwell's enjoy the conversation and I'll be back for breakfast."

The horses were fed and brushed and the chickens were eating and the eggs were collected. The hands were leaving the field kitchen and some headed out to check cattle that were grazing all over the mountain while others worked around the houses and barns performing maintenance and general upkeep. Will saddled Blaze and had him ready to work the mountain as soon as breakfast was finished. He ran into Mary as she ran from the garden with a cup in her hand.

"Mary, what are you up to now?"

"Can't talk, dad, I'm in a hurry."

"Where are you off to, girl?"

"The kitchen. I have to get Pa some more coffee."

"Who's Pa?"

"The old one."

Will walked out into the garden and found his grandfather laughing and in a very happy mood.

"What are you laughing about, Pa?"

"That great granddaughter of mine is a pistol, isn't she. Someone has taught her well 'cause she can talk and work at the same time. We need to have her up here all the time."

"You might change your mind after she's been here for a while. Come on, let's eat breakfast."

Noon found Will and his father, Josh, in the lower meadows of the mountain high above the ranch house checking on the well being of their cattle. They all seemed in good health and by the time of the first snow, they would be fat and ready for market. As they rode Will talked of the drawings he had found and of Tessa's cattle ranch. They decided his father would have to look at it in person before he could make an honest appraisal of the idea. At least the idea created the need for his mother and father to come down from their mountain home to the desert floor for a visit. Their survey of the herd on the lower meadow completed, they started down toward the house.

The sound of a rifle shot brought them from conversation to full alert and Josh pulled his Henry rifle from its scabbard. A second shot rang out and both father and son dove from their horses to the ground.

"Any ideas where those shots came from, son?"

"No. I'm going to work my way over to those rocks to our right and try to find the shooter. Find some cover."

"Right. Just let me know if you see someone. It might be one of the hands shooting at a mountain lion or coyote."

"The bullets came our way, dad. I don't think it's someone who works for you. They know you're up here today."

Will crawled across the meadow to the rocks for cover and a vantage point. He scanned the area but found no movement or sign of someone hiding. Another shot rang out and the bullet hit close to his father, but the shooter had made a mistake. He had fired with the barrel of his rifle in the open and Will saw the muzzle flash.

"Dad. Can you hear me?"

"Yes. We gotta get this guy. That last shot was really close."

"The rocks to the left. About a hundred yards up from you. I saw the muzzle flash."

"I'll work my way around to his right and you take the left."

Another shot rang out as Josh worked his way around to the right and into the pines that circled the meadow. From the cover of a massive pine, he searched the rocks where Will said the shots came from, but saw nothing. He moved closer to the rocks and suddenly saw movement. He shouldered the Henry and fired and the bullet ricocheted around the rocks.

Will, approaching from the shooters left, saw movement and fired in to the rocks. They had him in a cross fire and he had no hope of escape. The would be assassin bolted from his perch and ran for his horse. Will fired again and Josh did the same and the man fell to the ground.

Both Josh and Will approached the downed man cautiously for he still might be able to use his side arm. When they found the body he was lying face down in the dirt, and when Will rolled him over he found he was still alive.

"It is one of my riders, Will. You were right, but we're lucky to be alive. I saw this boy kill a mountain lion on the run at one hundred and fifty yards. If he wanted us dead, we would be."

"Why would he be shooting at you? You and him have a run in?"

"No, in fact he asked for some time off to visit his folks over in Texas. I wasn't expecting him back for another two weeks."

"Who is it?"

"His name is John Hartley. You must remember him. He's been with us for about five years. Get his horse and we'll try to get him down the hill and get him patched up."

"Dad, he tried to kill you."

"No. I don't know why he shot at us. but if he'd wanted us dead, we would be. He wasn't trying to kill us, just get us out of the area."

As Will went to gather up his horse, John began to stir and regained consciousness. He opened his eyes and saw Josh bending over him.

"Mr. Tidwell...."

"Don't try to talk, son. You got two bullet holes in ya and we're takin' ya down the mountain to a doctor."

"Gotta talk, sir. I'm sorry for shootin' at ya. I want to apologize before I die so I can leave with a clear conscience."

"Easy, boy, you're going to be all right. Just hold on. Will's gone for your horse and we'll have you out of here in a hurry."

"No, there's not much time. I can tell I'm done for. Please listen to what I have to say."

Josh nodded and the boy continued.

"We robbed a bank over by Fort Sumner and my share of the money is in my saddlebags. Make sure the money gets returned, will ya? No one was hurt when we did it, but I want the money returned. I never shoulda got mixed up in this mess and I've got what I deserve."

"You said we, John. Who was with you when you robbed the bank?"

"Bob Simons and Walt Boyer were with me. They work on your wife's parents place. I met them in Lincoln. I never should have listened…." His eyes grew wide and Josh heard a gurgling sound and then his head rolled to the side. They would take his body down the mountain, but there would be no reason to hurry.

As Josh and Will rode in, the sun was setting and most of the hands were in from their days work and they gathered around when they saw the dead man tied across his saddle. Bonnie and Tessa ran from the house to find out what had happened. Josh called for all hands to gather round for he would explain what happened only once. Grandma Rebecca kept Mary in the house as Grandpa Liam went out to hear what happened.

"It's John Hartley tied across the saddle. He took a shot at me and Will up in the high meadow and we went after him. We didn't know who it was until we shot him. He asked for time off to visit his parents but admitted he and two others used the time to rob a bank over by Fort Sumner. The proof of what I say is in his saddlebags. They're full of money. Tomorrow early we'll take him into town and turn him and the money over to the sheriff. That's it. Now get on about your business. As the hands went back to what they were doing earlier, Tessa moved to Will's side.

"Are you okay?" Tessa asked. "It's so terrible. You could have been killed."

"I'm fine and really never was in danger. What dad didn't say was that John was an expert shot and if he had wanted us dead, we would be. He just wanted us out of the area so he wouldn't be found. Now let me take care of the body. We'll put him in the root cellar for the night. It's cool there and will help keep the body. Go on now and let Mary know everything is okay. I love you and I'll be right in."

Josh took the saddlebags and handed them to Bonnie to take in the house and then walked with Will and John's horse to the root cellar.

The following morning Josh found Will sitting at the kitchen table cleaning his gun. Will had made coffee and Josh poured himself a cup and then sat down at the table with his son.

"You expecting trouble today, son?"

"You never know. The sheriff will probably want some help rounding up the other two that were with John. I figure I should be in on the end of this as we're the one's that found out about it. I sure would want the help if I were him."

"Maybe you're right, but you won't go alone. We make a pretty good pair to go up against."

"Thanks, dad. I knew you'd understand. Just don't say anything around Tessa or Mary. I don't want them to worry. Mary will probably want to tag along, so she'll be upset enough when I tell her no."

"I don't know about that, son. Mary and dad have become inseparable and she'll probably want to stay with him."

"I hope so."

Rebecca and Bonnie came into the kitchen followed closely by Tessa. They saw Will finishing with his gun and watched him slip it into his holster.

"Strange time to be cleaning a gun, so early in the morning. Expecting some kind of trouble, are we?"

"Not at all, Grandma. Better clean than dirty, isn't that what you always say? Well, look at it like this, at some time in my life I did listen." And they all laughed.

"Where's Mary? Is she sleeping in? That's not like her," Will said.

"Wherever your grandpa is that's where you'll find Mary. They're probably out with the chickens or in the garden," Bonnie said. "I'm so glad they get along so well. She's just what this family has always needed."

"And what might that be?" Josh asked.

"Some new female family blood. You know, Josh, something I always wanted but couldn't seem to get."

"Oh, so now it's my fault. I don't think so."

They all laughed and were happy to see Tessa laughing too. She truly fit right into the family and everyone was happy to have her.

With breakfast finished, Will went to the barn and saddled the horses he and his father would ride and the horse that would carry John Hartley's body to town. Will could see his father coming out of the house with Mary on his heels and knew she would have a problem if not allowed to ride with them. But as Liam came out of the house she ran to his side and asked what they would work on today.

"I told you son, those two are a pair. They'll keep each other busy all day. Let's get John and get on the road."

As they rode past the house toward the road to town, Tessa appeared in the yard. Will stopped and leaned over in the saddle and gave her a kiss.

"You be careful today and stay away from trouble. I love you and want you here with me," she said in a pleading voice. "I plan on us living a long and happy life together."

"Don't worry. We're just going to town to see the sheriff and the rest will be up to him. We'll be home soon." As he rode away, he hoped she believed him.

Lincoln seemed to be growing bigger every time he went to town and the sight of a dead man being brought in gathered a crowd and they followed the riders all the way to the sheriff's office. The big two story brown building on the west end of town housed the sheriff's office, court house, and town hall and it was there that they stopped. The sheriff stepped from his office as they approached.

"Morning, Tidwell. What have you gotten me into now? Who's tied to the horse."

"Morning, Dornan. I think we better talk in your office in private. Will, I don't think you've met Sheriff Dornan. Dornan, my son Will.

"Nice to meet you, son. You want privacy, let's get in the office."

Josh explained what had happened and what they had been told by John before he died and it was decided they should get after the other two bank robbers before they found out what was going on. Right now, the sheriff, Josh and Will had the advantage and they wanted to keep it that way.

The Davis Ranch had been run by Len Dawson for years and Josh could see no reason to replace the foreman when his wife's parents were killed. Len saw the men riding toward his ranch office and went out to meet them.

"Morning Mr. Tidwell. What are you doing out this way, sheriff? Have some of the boys been tryin' your patience in town?"

"No, Len, this is something a lot more serious. Let's go in your office and talk about it."

"You still got Bob Simons and Walt Boyer workin' for you?"

"Yeah. But they just got back today. They took some time off and been gone for over a week. Don't know where they took off too."

"I do. They were over by Fort Sumner and they robbed a bank. Josh here just brought in the body of the third member of their gang and before he died he told Josh and Will here what happened and who did it."

"What is it you want here? The men are all out working."

"Where did you send Simons and Boyer to work today?"

"They're working the upper pastures today countin' stock and checkin' water holes."

"They could be anywhere on that mountain, boys. We'll have to wait 'til they come in this evening." The sheriff took off his hat and scratched his head and said, "What do you think, Josh?"

"Guess you're right, but I can't sit around here all day doin' nothin'. I got a lot of work to do before the sun sets," Josh said in answer to the sheriff.

"I'll stick around, dad. Just make sure you tell Tessa where I am so she won't worry. I can ride around and see if I can find them, and if not, I'll visit with friends I meet as I ride. But, you remember to tell Tessa where I am, okay?"

"I'll tell her and I'll be back over here around four or five o'clock. The hands should start coming in about that time. They know me and they know Will and they won't think anything is up if they see us. But you, sheriff, you better stay in the office where you won't be seen or they'll know something is wrong."

"Good idea, Josh. From the office I can see the whole area. When you show up, if all goes well, I'll know where they are and we can surprise them and take them in without firing a shot."

With plans made for later in the day, Josh decided to leave for home and get to the chores he had to take care of before he could come back for Simons and Boyer. He touched the brim of his hat and rode toward home. Will walked over to the ranch kitchen and made himself a bacon sandwich with the left overs from the mornings breakfast. One of the young girls that worked in the kitchen asked if he would like some coffee and when he nodded his head, brought him a cup. As he ate the sandwich he watched Len Dawson and the way he worked with his men. He asked and they did for the hands knew he wouldn't ask them to do something he wouldn't do himself. Will thought of Sheriff Dornan sitting in the ranch office and decided to take him a sandwich and cup of coffee to help him pass the time. Blaze was tied in front of the office and after delivering the sandwich and coffee untied the horse and walked him toward the barn. He looked for and found a leather punch which he used to punch a new hole in Blaze's bridal to loosen it a bit for a better fit. He then stuck his foot in the stirrup and climbed into the saddle and rode past the trail to town and up the mountain to where Len Dawson's men worked.

The trail up the mountain was steep so Will went slowly to allow Blaze to catch his breath and not tire to quickly. He thought he would have to retire the old gelding soon for he was getting old. He remembered General and Windy and how they had been turned out when they were retired and they wouldn't leave. Wherever his father went they went and it kept all three of them happy. He recalled the morning he found General lying down when he went in to feed the stock and how he never moved when he spoke to him. He had died during the night, but he had lived a full and happy life. Three weeks later Windy, the pinto, died and everyone in the family believed she died of a broken heart. Her best friend had left without her and she didn't understand why. Will decided he would turn Blaze out before he made his trip down the mountain to the Parker Ranch.

The day seemed to pass slowly and the men Will had talked to hadn't seen Simons or Boyer since breakfast that morning. So as the sun changed from east to west he started back down the mountain to the ranch office and Sheriff Dornan. His father would be there soon and then the fireworks would start for there was no doubt in Will's mind that Simon's more than Boyer wouldn't give up without a fight.

Will stopped at a clearing that gave a good view of the ranch house and other facilities that made up the Davis Ranch. The foreman's house and the bunk house, the field kitchen and the barns, the stables and the tack house could all be seen from this vantage point. It was too bad, Will thought, that the main ranch house sat empty for it was an immaculate home. Mrs. Davis had really good taste when it came to home furnishings, but not so good when it came to son-in-laws. As he rode on down the mountain he thought he would have to bring Tessa to this spot for it was absolutely beautiful.

Will tied Blaze to the roof support of the ranch office and walked in to talk to Sheriff Dornan and found him watching the men as they came in from their work. He turned as Will walked in and asked, "Where have you been, son? I'm about to starve here and you're out runnin' around the mountains. Think ya could get me a sandwich or a pie or anything to eat. I'm starvin."

"I'll see what I can do, but why didn't you get one of the girls to bring you something to eat. That's what they do here. They feed people who are hungry. Next time, just ask and they'll make sure you don't go hungry. Has my dad arrived yet?"

"Haven't seen him yet, but Dawson pointed out one of the boys we're looking for. We'll just have to wait for the other one to show up, him and your father. We could take him now, but it might get the other one suspicious and he might take off. Let's just wait and see what happens."

Josh rode in as Will left the ranch office and headed for the field kitchen. He was after food for the sheriff and was in a hurry. He didn't want to get caught with his hands full of food when he needed it full of gun.

Josh saw Boyer as he walked into the office and the sheriff had seen him too. One down and one to go Josh thought as he closed the office door.

"Has Simons come in yet or are we still waiting for him to show up," Josh asked as he pulled his Navy Colt from its holster and checked each of the six chambers. "No matter what happens, we finish this tonight. I don't want this kind of thing thought to be appropriate behavior for Tidwell riders," he said in a humorous way and they laughed.

"Something strange is going on around here," Boyer said to himself.

He wasn't a big man and his early grey hair made him look older than his actual age. He wore a black leather hat and sported a grey handlebar mustache which when nervous he continually twisted the ends. When Simons rode in Boyer signaled him to meet him in the barn. When the two met, he told Simons of his concerns.

"Listen Simons, something strange is going on here. Mr. Tidwell is here and his son has been here all day. And I caught a glimpse of who I think was the sheriff in the office. Now why do you suppose they are all here today. And where was John Hartley? He was to meet us tonight, right? I tell ya, there's something goin' on here and I think we're goin' to be a big part of it."

"Bull, you just worry too much. Just walk around like you own the place and everything will be okay." Bob Simons was a tall young man and was known to have a quick temper. His friends said it was because of his red curly hair that he had such an Irish temper. He was also known for his expertise with a gun and his fast draw.

Walt Boyer was a worrier and everyone that knew him knew he was always on edge. He was no gunman and no one had ever seen him in a fight. If it weren't for Simons he would probably have been a loner. This day, however, it seemed he might pull his mustache out by the roots.

When leaving the barn the two men went in opposite directions making it harder for them to be caught. When the sheriff stepped from the office and called his name, Simons bolted in the direction Boyer had gone.

Josh called to Will who had worked his way out of the office and around the field kitchen toward the bunkhouse. "Take the back of the bunkhouse, Will, and be ready. If they come out that way, they'll probably be shootin', so be careful. What do you think, sheriff? Shall we take them on rushing straight in or have you a different idea? I'm ready, so let's do it."

"All right, Mr. Tidwell. Straight in. Let's go."

As Josh kicked the door open and entered the bunkhouse with Colt in hand and Dornan right behind him Boyer and Simons went out the back.

The next thing he heard was four shots from the back. As he made his way out the back door, he saw two bodies laying on the ground, but he didn't see Will.

Will watched as the two men ran from the back door of the bunkhouse with their guns in hand. As they saw him they aimed and fired in his direction. Will drew the engraved Peace Maker and fired twice and the two men fell to the ground dead.

"Will, where are you?" his father called.

The sheriff rolled the two men over and found they had both been shot in the chest and probably through the heart. It was evident why neither had said a word, they never had a chance.

Will walked out the back door of the bunkhouse and said, "You know, dad, you have to pay for the doors you tore down and we'll have to patch them up before we leave for home."

Sheriff Dornan found the money they took from the bank in spare saddlebags that hung in their personal lockers and asked if he could borrow a wagon to get the bodies back to town. Their was a reward out for the bank robbers and he asked Will where he wanted him to send the money.

"You killed 'em, boy. You get the reward. If your dad killed 'em I'd give the money to him. See how it's done."

"Sheriff Dornan, we'll split the money three ways. You get one third and a third goes to my dad. My share of the money I want to go to the padre at the mission church. I know he will put it to good use."

Chapter Sixteen
Desert Bound

When Josh and Will returned home daylight was fading and the stars would soon be coming into view. As usual, the family gathered around the kitchen table to hear of the deeds of the day and Josh kept pointing at Will and telling them to ask the younger Mr. Tidwell what happened. Will simply said that the two men ran out of the bunkhouse shooting and he protected himself. That was all there was to it. Now, he said, we'll hear no more of it.

The following morning Will again sat in the kitchen waiting for his father to come in and while he sat he talked with his mother and grandmother.

"You know, Will," his mother said, "it wouldn't take much to get Tessa and Mary to stay here."

"You think so, huh. I think you forget she has a ranch and cattle of her own. And she has men, as have we, that work and depend on her for a living. I'm not sure she's ready to give all that up yet."

"Show her around some more and see what she has to say, then talk to her."

"I would like to show her your parents house if it's okay. No one lives there and it seems such a waste to leave it empty. I found a place above the main house on the side of the mountain where you can see the whole layout of the ranch house and other buildings. I want to show her that first and then the house. Then we'll see what she has to say."

"It would make everyone here happy if you decided to stay here on the mountain with us as we have grown quickly to love both Tessa and Mary and I'm sure they feel the same about us. They have always fit right in and been a part of the family. See what you can do about this, okay," Grandma Rebecca asked.

Bonnie walked to a drawer at the far end of the kitchen, opened it and took the keys to her parents house out. As she handed the keys to Will she said, "Show Tessa the whole house, Will. If you do she will fall in love with it and it should help make her decision to stay."

Mary walked into the kitchen from out doors and said, "Pa would like this cup filled again, please, but not so much sugar this time he said. Hi, dad. Where's mom?"

"Mary, would you mind if your mother and I went for a ride today by ourselves? I have some things I want to show her I really don't think you would be interested in. I want to......"

"It's okay with me, dad. Besides, I couldn't go anyway. Pa and I are too busy and we still have a lot of work to do. You two go and have fun doing all that kissing and stuff. I'm needed here. Thanks for the coffee. I gotta go before Pa gets any thirstier."

"I'm needed here," she said. "She doesn't realize how true her words really are," Bonnie said.

"Okay, I'll see what I can do. I'll ask dad if it's all right for me to take today off."

When everyone was seated at the breakfast table Bonnie said, "My son is taking today off and showing his wife around the countryside, Josh. Have the boys hitch up the surrey and have it ready to go when they're ready to leave. And you tell them I said they better do it right or they'll catch heck from me."

"Yes, ma'am. It'll be ready when they are, you can bet on that," Josh said. "Is it okay if I eat breakfast or should I go do it right now? What ever makes you happy is what you'll get." Everyone laughed at his attempt to be funny, but they also knew that Bonnie had meant every word she said. She didn't often make her demands known and usually went along with the majority, but this was something she really wanted and she wasn't going to let this opportunity to have her family near pass.

The ride around the countryside began with all the places Will liked to escape to when he was a boy. At each site, he would tell Tessa what it was that made the place special to him. A little before noon they were at the lower of the high meadows where hundreds of long-horn cattle grazed on the lush deep green mountain grass. As they started down again Tessa said, "It is really beautiful here, Will. Mary and I have had such a wonderful time while we've been here and your family has treated us as if they've known us our whole lives. I'm sure they love us as much as we love them. Mary has taken to Pa and he has taken to her as if she were his own. I know it's time to go back down to our ranch, but we'll have to come back up often."

"You've seen the mountain when the weathers been nice, but what about when the snow is five feet deep and it's fifteen below zero. How will you like the mountain then?"

"I know it gets cold. Your mom and grandma told me all about how the winters can seem so much longer than they really are. I'm thinking more about family than the weather. Besides, I'm sure the cold in the winter is no worse than the heat in the summer down home."

Will drove the surrey up the side of the mountain to where he had looked down on the Davis Ranch the day before. When Tessa saw the home and out buildings through the trees she asked, "Who lives down there, Will? What a beautiful setting. This would make a very nice painting."

"No one lives down there now. It's my mothers parents home and no one has lived in the house since they were killed. Want to see what it looks like on the inside?"

"Oh yes, Will."

"Let's go then. I have the keys so we'll take a look."

The house itself was built of river rock and wood and the roof of cedar shakes. The outside was well manicured and the many flower beds evenly spaced across the front of the house spread all the colors of the rainbow within their borders. There were four fireplaces within the outer walls of the home, one in the grand room, one in the library, one in the master bedroom and one in the kitchen. The windows were covered with heavy, colorful curtains that shaded the rooms in the summer and kept the cold out in the winter. The great room was filled with leather sofas, leather chairs, ornate tables and lamps and longhorn horns mounted and hung above the fireplace. The entire house was furnished by someone who knew well what furnishings went with which room.

"Why doesn't some family live here, Will?" Tessa asked.

"Mom always said it would take someone very special to her for her to allow the house to be occupied again. She feels as we do, though, in that she thinks it's a shame for it to sit here empty. Anything else you want to see here? Oh, yeah, there's a basement where they kept all the canned goods and the attic has a full floor in it. The stairway off the kitchen goes up there and the door beneath the stairs goes to the basement. You want to see them?"

"No, I've seen enough. This is a real home and makes mine look like a home for the poor. I've seen all I need to see and I'm ready to go whenever you are."

"There is nothing at all wrong with your home, Tessa. You have to remember they have a few more years of setting these places up than you have. You've done a wonderful job with your house for the amount of time you have to work on it. Mom and Grandma Rebecca don't run a ranch like you do. That's dads job. They have most of the day to work at getting the houses the way they want them. But you have had to do it all and as I see it, you've done an excellent job."

"You really love being here with your family, don't you?"

"Sure, but I'd be gone in an instant if I thought you were unhappy here. We'd be down the mountain and back into the desert to your ranch as fast as I could get us there. You are my wife and I love you. I would never do anything to make you unhappy."

Tessa wrapped her arms around Will's arm and squeezed it tight. He always knew what to say to make her feel better and cheer her up.

"Let's head back to your mom's house before it gets too late. I know you have to be starving. You haven't eaten since breakfast. Thank you for sharing your childhood with me, Will. I had a real nice time today and would like to do it again sometime soon."

The trail to the Parker Ranch went right by the entrance to the Davis Ranch and as Tessa drove the surrey by the entrance she paused and looked down the long tree lined entry. She liked the way the trees on each side of the drive formed a tunnel and shaded the way into the ranch. Mary rode Bullet near the surrey to see where her mother was looking.

"What are you looking for, mom?"

"Nothing really. Just thinking about the way things could be compared to the way they are right now."

"What did you say?" Mary asked not knowing that her mother was talking to herself more than her.

"Let's get going or we'll never make it home," Tessa said and moved the surrey to the center of the trail that led to their desert home.

Will could see something was bothering his wife, but made no mention of it. He knew if she wanted to talk about it she would let him know. The farther they went from Lincoln the more irritated she became and finally wanted to talk about it. She stopped the surrey and called for Will.

"Will, tie your horse to the back of the surrey and ride with me for a while, okay. I want to talk to you."

Will did as she asked and climbed into the seat of the surrey with her. He didn't know what was bothering her, but knew he was about to find out.

"Will, you really put a lot of worth in family, right?" I've never had any family other than Russ and Mary. When I was a kid I lived with my grandmother and she wasn't anything like Rebecca or Bonnie, believe me. The time we have spent up here with your family has taught me a lot about being part of a real family and I want more of it."

"You are a part of the family, Tessa. When you married me, you married into the whole bunch. What is it you're really trying to say? Get it out and let's discuss it." Will put his arm around her and pulled her close. "Come on, out with it."

"I don't want to leave, Will. I like having family around and being able to help them so that their life is easier. And Mary, did you see how she acted when we told her it was time to go home. She thought she was home just as I did and we both loved being part of it."

"Are you sure about this? It'll be a big change for you because you'll no longer run a ranch or be the boss. You'll be a wife, mother, home maker and all around beautiful lover. Think you can live with that?

And what about your place in the desert and the people that keep it running and make you money, what about them? I'm sure you'll want to see they're taken care of."

"Oh, Will, what are we going to do? I'm so confused I don't know which way to go."

"Just take your time and weigh both sides and see which one carries the most weight. Only you can decide which would make you happier."

"Okay, I'll think about it. But you have to get back on your horse and let me ride alone. When you're near I think of things better left to later in the day." She smiled and gave him a hug.

Darkness had fallen by the time they got home and a full moon was rising over the mountain they had just come down. It cast long shadows across the square between the house and barn. Mary had grown tired and Bullet, tied to the back of the surrey, watched over his young owner who slept curled up in their baggage. Tessa brought the surrey to a stop and climbed down as Maria came from the house to meet them. Will picked Mary up from the baggage and carried her to her room and Maria put her to bed. While Will took the horses and the surrey to the barn and settled them for the night, Tessa cornered Maria and asked her if she would like to move up on the mountain.

"Oh my goodness, Tessa. I thought I would live the rest of my life right here with you and Mary. What have I done to make you want to send me away?"

"No, no, Maria. I'm not sending you away. Mary and I might move and if we do we want you to move with us. You are part of our family and always will be. We want to keep you with us."

"What does Mr. Will think about me going with you?" Maria asked as Will walked into the house.

"Mr. Will wants you to do what makes you happy. If you want to move, we'll be happy to have you with us. If you decide to go another way, you will have my blessing," Will said as he entered the room where they talked. "I'm hungry and I'm headed for the kitchen. Any one else hungry?"

"There is some cobbler in the oven and it should be done. Wait just a moment and I'll get some for you," Maria said. "I want to tell Mrs. Will something and then I'll be there." As Will disappeared toward the kitchen, Maria continued. "You know you and Mary are my reason for living, so where ever you go I will go and as long as I am with you and Mary I will be happy."

"Good, we've got that settled. Now let's go get Mr. Will something to eat before he starves to death," Tessa said as she and Maria walked to the kitchen.

"Will, remember when I met you in Las Cruces to bring you home, but we spent the night. Remember when we were having dinner and I introduced you to Walter Ramsey, my neighbor? I think I'll contact him and see if he really wants to buy the ranch. Maria has said she will move with us and I'll try to make a deal that allows the rest of the workers to keep their jobs here. We'll just have to wait and see what he says. I've talked with Mary and I've talked with Maria and now I'm talking to you. I think it's been decided that if Walter still wants to buy, we're going to move. We can use the money we get for this ranch to build ourselves a new home on the mountain. What do you think?"

"I think you need to save your money and slow down and let things fall into place. You don't have to buy or build a new home. Mom has already said that if we decide to move back to the mountain, we can have her parents home. I know you really liked that house and there's plenty of room for Maria too. But let's not get our hopes up until we talk to Mr. Ramsey."

"I'm going to bed and you better be there pretty quick, you hear. I like having you close no matter where we live."

When Tessa left the kitchen Maria walked near to Will and said, "Mr. Will, I know Tessa and Mary a long time and I never see them happy before like now. I'm glad you found her."

"Thank you, Maria. I'm glad I found them too. Why don't you go get some rest. I'll clean up after myself. I'll see you in the morning. Good night." He finished his cobbler, cleaned up his dish and spoon and turned out the lamps and went to check on Mary. He blew out the candles and turned out the rest of the lamps and disappeared into his bedroom and was with Tessa.

Walter Ramsey's ranch was about ten or twelve miles from the Parker Ranch and when Tessa and Will drove into his yard he was in the barn. His house was just what was necessary to survive, four walls and a door to keep the cold wind out in the winter. The barn was much nicer than the house. Will thought it was obvious why he wanted Tessa's place, he wanted a nice house. He was dressed for work and his clothes looked like he had been hard at work for days. He removed his gloves to shake their hands and wiped his forehead with the sleeve of his shirt.

"What brings you over this way, Mrs. Parker?"

"It's Mrs. Tidwell now, Walter. We dropped by to see if you were still serious about purchasing my ranch. If you are, I think I'm in the mood to sell."

"Of course I'm still interested. I need more grass and more water for my cattle. How much ya askin' for the place? I'm not rich, ya know."

"I know you know its value. They told me in town that you've been checking land prices. But you have to remember this one comes with everything. It's a working ranch complete with cattle, a foreman, seven hands, and three field kitchen workers. I want it to be written into the sales contract that they will be kept on the ranch and not let go. Does that sound fair to you? So then, what will you offer me for my ranch?"

"I believe a fair price for your ranch is one hundred thousand dollars. What do you say?"

"Mr. Ramsey, my wife has come to you first because you've shown an interest in the past in the ranch. You have to remember there are over fifteen hundred steers on the ranch nearly ready to ship to market as well as the stock necessary to replenish the herd and run the place. It has a home for you and facilities to house and feed your hired help. This isn't some place you'll have to start from scratch and it's over ten thousand acres with a lot of grass. So, if you intend to bore us with ridiculous offers, we can go into Las Cruces and find any number of serious buyers that will make offers that don't insult us."

"You got a lot of your granddad in you, son. He didn't take too much to haggling either. Okay, I'll give you two hundred and twenty-five thousand for your ranch and not a cent more. And I'll sign a note saying all the workers can stay. With the extra cattle and ground to keep an eye on, I'll need the help anyway. And I really like Maria's cookin'."

"That's real nice, Walter, but Maria is moving with me. Sorry, but you'll have three cooks in the field kitchen and they work the garden too."

"Then we have a deal, Mr. Tidwell?"

"Tessa says yes, so we have a deal. Tomorrow around noon we can meet at the bank in town and sign the papers. When will you want to take possession?"

"As soon as possible. I wasn't joking when I said I needed the water and the grass. One of my wells on the upper plain northwest of the house went dry. We'll start digging it deeper tomorrow."

"Mr. Ramsey, if we have no problems with the paperwork or you coming up with the cash, I'll show ya how to grow enough hay for all your stock. You'll have to invest a little effort, but it can be done. I guarantee it. I would imagine it should also double the worth of the ranch."

Josh told Mr. Ramsey of the maps he had found and how drilling the wells and digging the required ditches would allow for the irrigation of a thousand acres of hay. The thought of that much feed for his cattle was more than enough to seal the deal and bring about the rapid sale of the Parker Ranch.

Leaving the ranch to move up on the mountain didn't have the effect on Tessa and Mary Will thought it would have. When at the bank in Las Cruces to sign the deed of sale there had been no hesitation on Tessa's part and she was more than happy when she received the cash promised for her ranch. When leaving the bank and heading for the last time to her desert home she said, "Will, I've never made a deal before that I was so sure was the right thing to do."

Chapter Seventeen
A Family Together

Three weeks later two wagons full of household goods made their way up the mountain in the direction of Lincoln and the Tidwell Ranch. Traveling with the two wagons were William, Tessa and Mary Tidwell and Maria Cruz and they were headed to their new home on the mountain.

Like his father before him, Will had learned that family came first and their welfare foremost in his thoughts. He had found that for which he left home to find was not a place, it was a person. For the first time in his life he was truly happy and his wife and daughter were what brought that happiness to fruition.

Four generations of Tidwell's would live on the ranch that was their home. Like his father and his grandfather, he too would raise his family on the mountain in Lincoln County, New Mexico Territory.

CPSIA information can be obtained at www.ICGtesting.com
Printed in the USA
LVOW130843160213

320360LV00001B/2/P